INHERITED HOLIDAY

M. ROBINSON

M. ROBINSON
© 2024 Inherited Holiday by M. Robinson

Interior Formatting by Swoonworthy Designs
Cover Designer: Ya'll That Graphics
Editing:4 Indies Editor: Jenny Sims

Dear Santa,

This holiday romance is for anyone who prefers The Grinch because he has something that grows three times the size for you...

And by that,

I mean his cock.

PROLOGUE

NICHOLAS

"What the hell do you mean by I've inherited Mistletoe Town?" I argued with my grandfather's estate attorney.

I was completely thrown off guard by the unexpected reading of his will.

"Exactly what I just said, Mr. Saint Clair. The town is now yours. You own it."

I sat there dumbfounded, utterly confused by the turn of events. The last time I stepped foot in that godforsaken Christmas town was when I left everyone in it thirteen years ago. I never looked back.

"You can't be serious, Alfred."

"Quite the contrary, sir."

"Well, I'm urging you to reconsider."

"It's not personal." He shook his head. "He's just looking out for the future of his legacy."

"Not personal, my ass! It couldn't get any more personal than what he's demanding of me."

I took a deep breath and cracked my neck, feeling the throbbing strain from my pulsating jugular vein. This man knew how to push every one of my buttons and did it without hesitation. Even from the grave. Now he was pushing me to the brink of insanity, and I was just supposed to sit back and obey like a lapdog.

Inhaling another deep, solid breath, I snapped, "And what if I don't want it?"

He shrugged as if what he had just informed me of didn't turn my life upside down.

I muttered under my breath, "I can't believe this."

"Mr. Saint Clair," he stressed, sliding the documents over to me. "It's what your grandfather wanted."

"No," I snapped again. "What my grandfather wanted was to control me, and since he couldn't do it while he was alive, he's now demanding it when he's dead."

I couldn't believe he thought I'd just bend at his will like he was simply asking me to take a meeting with a client and not alter the course of my entire future in such a drastic way.

The audacity of my grandfather knew no bounds.

He'd always been relentless in his pursuit, determined to make whatever he thought was right happen, no matter what or who it affected. The sad part was we were one and the same. I was exactly like him. For the first time in my life, I had no idea what the outcome would be, and I hated that more than anything.

"We all know what you're capable of, Mr. Saint Clair," he coaxed, pulling me away from my reckless thoughts.

"You think he's doing this to you when, in reality, he's doing this *for you*."

"You're being unreasonable and need to consider the possibilities."

I contemplated his statement for a moment before quickly

realizing this wasn't a debate between my grandfather and me but an ambush from beyond the grave.

I narrowed my eyes at him, taken aback by what he meant.

Alfred nodded to the folder in front of me. "There's a letter in there from your grandfather." With that, he abruptly stood and walked toward my office door. "I'll be outside once you're ready, and then we can go over all the logistics. However, we don't have a lot of time. You're due in Mistletoe Town this afternoon to begin this year's festivities and meet your new employees."

"I can't pick up and go like that," I bit. "I have deadlines to meet with my clients and their homes."

I was a general contractor with a thriving business. We focused on new builds and some remodels. I made a name for myself without the help of my family, and it wasn't something I was going to give up without one hell of a fight. I had no interest in taking this on, whether he demanded it of me or not.

"Well, I hate to break it to you, but you'll have to figure it out. Like I said, you're due in town this afternoon."

"I don't give a shit."

"Then you're going to be responsible for all the children and their families not getting the Christmas experience your family has lived up to for decades. You want that guilt hanging over your head?"

"What the hell?" I stared at him in disbelief. "What am I, Santa, now?"

"Yes, sir." He adamantly nodded. "The town is now your responsibility. Without you, it won't run."

"That's a lot of pressure to put on someone who has no idea how to run that town to begin with. Especially just a few days before Christmas. This is ridiculous! You're telling me my grandfather expects me to drop everything I've worked so hard for, for what? A town I hate and a holiday I can't stand."

"Yes… Mr. Saint Clair, we're all aware of your distaste for a joyful time, but it's what your grandfather wanted."

"And my family? My parents? My siblings? What do they all have to say about this?"

"They agree."

I jerked back, more confused than I was before. "You have got to be kidding me."

"As I said…" He gestured to the envelope in my hand. "You're due in Mistletoe Town this afternoon."

He quickly turned and left, closing the door behind him. I don't know how long I sat there in a state of shock. I was mostly pissed that my grandfather was getting the last word on an argument that made me leave Mistletoe in the first place.

I growled in frustration as I ripped open the envelope to read what his last words were to me. As soon as I saw the four sentences in big, black, bold font, I scoffed in disagreement and threw the paper in the middle of my desk.

There it lay, mocking me…

ALL I WANT FOR CHRISTMAS IS FOR MY GRANDSON TO FINALLY COME HOME.
IT'S TIME, NICHOLAS.

MISTLETOE TOWN IS YOURS NOW, DON'T DISAPPOINT ME. IT'S WHAT YOUR GRANDMOTHER WANTS.

"Fuck… of course he'd pull that card," I rasped to myself, pressing the intercom button for my secretary, Sarah, down the hall. "I will need you to clear the rest of my week."

"Mr. Saint Clair, you have—"

"I know."

She hesitated for a second as if she knew where I was going with this. I never canceled work. Come rain or shine, I always met my commitments. I was a workaholic, and I preferred it that way. Honestly, staying busy kept me sane. Like my grandfather constantly reminded me, "A body in motion stays in motion." That was my regime.

Sarah questioned, "What do I tell them?"

Leaning my head back against the leather chair, I stared up at the ceiling. "I have an unexpected family emergency."

She lightly gasped. "Does that mean—"

"Yeah…" I deeply sighed.

"I'm going back to hell."

CHAPTER 1

NOELLE

The first time I met Nicholas Saint Clair, I was fourteen years old, and he was fifteen. After years of living overseas with my dad while he was on active duty in the military, he was finally able to retire, and we moved to Mistletoe Town, where all your Christmas dreams come true.

My mom passed away when I was six, and I couldn't wait to move to a place where I'd suddenly feel her presence everywhere I went. My mom grew up in this town and dreamed of moving us there once my dad retired. Even after her unexpected death, my father followed through with their plan.

At first, I thought it would be an issue for him, but I think it helped heal him. Now he spent most of his time traveling, but something about this town just brought out the best in people. From the moment I stepped off the airplane, I fell in love with everything about Mistletoe Town.

Everything, and I do mean everything, about this Hallmark place was magical.

From the pristine landscaping everywhere you went to the perfectly designed neighborhoods and businesses that just screamed Christmas all year round, it was incredible. The charming aesthetic was right out of a holiday postcard or Hallmark movie. Tourists traveled from all over the world to experience the nostalgia that only this town could bring. It was contagious, even warming the coldest hearts.

Or so I thought...

The town truly was a sight to see, so to be able to actually call it home wasn't something I ever took for granted. The picturesque location had all four seasons every year. I personally was a fan of winter only because I loved Christmas with all my heart and soul.

I know that sounded corny, trust me. However, I didn't care. Christmas was a part of my identity, like my mom's. I took pride in carrying on her traditions from year to year and helping others create their own. From a young age, I had a passion for baking. I think it had something to do with the Woods genes and our sweet tooth.

I turned that hobby into a career, and I'd been the town baker for the past nine years. I started from the bottom and worked my way up. My dream was to eventually own this shop one day, but in the meantime, I treated it as if it were already mine. I took my job very seriously. Making memories with families year after year was one of my favorite things about my career.

Nothing was better than seeing a kid's face light up with the beauty and magic of this town. I loved every second of it. I guess you could say I was Mrs. Claus, and Mistletoe Town was The North Pole. Everyone knew each other, which meant there wasn't much for a personal life, but you could easily forget that once you experienced the true joy of Christmas like everyone should at least once in their lives.

Out of all the historic sites, my favorite was the library in the middle of the town square that housed all the greatest literary classics. I'd always been a book nerd. It was hard to make friends when we constantly moved, and I found companionship in the stories I read. To see four floors filled with novels by some of the greatest writers in history was a memory I'd never forget. I hung out there often, and that hadn't changed in the past fourteen years.

The truth was, Nicolas Saint Clair was my first real friend. You could even go as far as saying he was my best friend. But that was then, and this was now...

I hadn't seen or spoken to him since he left Mistletoe Town thirteen years ago, and now, he owned the town he ran away from.

Including my bakery.

His plane landed an hour ago, and it was only a matter of time before he'd step foot into my happy place, spinning it into a whirlwind. From the moment I heard the unexpected news, I couldn't think straight. It was unbelievable that his grandfather would leave his most prized possession to a man who didn't actually want it.

Especially when he could have left it to someone who genuinely did. Although I knew he was adamant about keeping it in their family because he turned down millions upon millions of dollars a year to investment buyers dying to get a piece of the pie. It became such a hopeless endeavor that investors stopped trying to take it from under him.

As much as I wanted to pretend to be unfazed by what was about to happen when Nicolas and I locked eyes for the first time after all these years, out of nowhere, I was hit with the memory of the first time we met.

It played out in my mind like it was happening right then and there.

An unfamiliar, rough voice asked, "You new here."

It was technically a question, but it came out more like a statement. In seconds, my eyes met his, and for a moment, I thought I imagined him, leaning against the bookcase with his arms crossed over his chest.

He instantly intrigued me. There was just something about him that piqued my interest.

"Is that a yes?" he added, arching an eyebrow. "Or does the Grinch have your undivided attention?"

I bit back a smile. He was talking about the book I was reading.

"Aren't you Nicholas Saint Clair?" I blurted.

I was never one for beating around the bush.

The Saint Clairs created this town decades ago and were basically royalty, but from what I heard, Nicholas kept to himself despite his family being who they were and loving every minute of the spotlight.

"I guess it depends on who you're asking."

I shrugged, not backing down. "I guess I'm asking you."

He smiled almost as if he enjoyed my response. "I'd say the Grinch and I have more in common than I do with the legacy of being a Saint Clair," he mocked, grinning. "Especially in this Christmas-obsessed town where nothing else matters but Santa Claus coming to town."

"Oh..." I jerked back, surprised by his outburst.

"Don't look at me like that," he ordered in a sharp tone, sitting in the chair in front of me.

My eyebrows pinched together. "Like what?"

"Like I just told you you're on the naughty list."

I snickered. I couldn't help it.

"But don't worry," he baited, leaning back into his seat. "I'm on that list every year."

Playing along, I stated, "You must have a lot of coal."

He grinned again. "It keeps my tools clean and nice and sharp."

"Your tools?"

"Yeah." He leaned forward, placing his elbows on the table. "I help fix and build things around town."

"Like a handyman?"

He nodded.

"Hmm... you didn't want to work at any of the businesses your family owns? I mean, they do run everything in this town."

I'd never forget what he said next. "If there's one thing you need to know about me, Noelle..."

I cocked my head to the side, realizing he knew my name too.

"Is that I don't do anything I don't want to. Especially when it comes to Mistletoe Town."

"Ugh!" I groaned, realizing I just stuck the cake mixer into the bowl when it was on. Flour suddenly flew everywhere, including in my face and on my body. "Great! Just great!"

Throwing the mixer on the ceramic counter, I quickly slid off my long-sleeved dress at the exact moment the door to my shop dinged open.

"Oh my God!" Instinctively, I shot around until my feet stopped dead in their tracks, almost giving me whiplash in the process. I came face-to-face with the guy who still haunted my dreams.

Nicholas's stare went wide, gawking at me like it was the first time he'd seen me in my lacy bra and panties. What made things worse was that I wore a black garter belt with stockings and heels. I was literally dressed in lingerie. What could I say? I was the kind of girl who loved to feel sexy in matching sets under her clothes.

When our eyes met, I was dragged to another place and time where he looked like a boy compared to the man he was now. Even after all this time, I was still physically affected by his mere presence. He was as handsome as ever with his bright, piercing green eyes and shining red hair and facial hair he was sporting. It only made him appear more distinguished and refined, but I knew better. Though it was the first time I'd seen him with a beard.

For the past thirteen years, I'd bent over backward for his family by running the bakery to the best of my ability. To see

Nicholas in the place I called my second home was a situation I never thought I'd find myself in.

As I took him in, my mind raced with questions I had no answers for. I hadn't seen him in so long, and there he was...

Standing right in front of me with a familiar yet unfamiliar expression and aura. It wasn't unusual to feel like I couldn't read him. If he didn't want me to know what he was thinking, feeling, wanting, or needing, then that was the end of it.

He was always in control of his emotions, even back then.

After what felt like forever, I finally broke the deafening silence between us, squealing, "Nicholas!" I grabbed my apron off the counter to cover my body, finally snapping out of whatever fog I was in.

He held his hands up in the air. "I... I..."

"Turn around!"

He immediately did. "Noelle, this isn't how I wanted us to—"

"I'm not normally naked in my bakery." I threw on the apron instead of just covering my body with it.

"Your bakery?" he questioned, turning around, but he took one look at me and gestured to my outfit. "This isn't any better, Elle."

He grinned in that shit-eating way I always hated.

Those five words had the effect he sought, making me remember the spark that had always been there between us and hadn't disappeared after all this time. We were best friends and did everything together, except we never crossed that line until a few weeks before he suddenly decided to leave Mistletoe Town a couple of months after graduating from high school.

He didn't call me.

He never texted me.

No letters.

No emails.

Not one word in thirteen years.

I thought about all of that as I abruptly left him standing there with that smug look, annoyed he was there in the first place. I changed into clean clothes, which were a pair of black overalls and a long-sleeved white shirt. I slipped on my Converse sneakers and made my way back out there. I always kept clothes in my office in case I had an unexpected baking explosion.

Focusing on the fact that I was no longer an impressionable teenager but a grown-ass woman, I marched in there with a different tune.

He announced, "I'm here—"

"I know why you're here."

We locked eyes for what felt like forever.

"Still sporting overalls, I see?"

"They're comfy for baking."

"Are you making me cookies? You know I'm a sucker for your mint chocolate chip."

I scoffed, rolling my eyes. "Hardly, Mr. Saint Clair."

"When you call me that, I look for my father."

"I'm just keeping it professional."

He walked toward me, and I stepped back.

"How professional can we be when I just saw you practically naked?"

"Anyway…" I changed the subject. "As I was saying, I know you're here."

He rubbed the back of his neck, avoiding my eyes for a moment. "I assume the whole town does."

"You, more than anyone, knows how fast news spreads here."

"Right." He glanced at me. "How could I forget?"

Unable to resist, I ask, "Wasn't that the point of you leaving?"

He tapered his gaze at me. "Now that's a loaded question if I've ever heard one, Elle."

"I have no interest in playing games with you, Mr. Saint Clair."

"I'll test my luck, then."

For the second time in a few short minutes, he shocked the shit out of me when he confessed,

"I'm so sorry, Noelle."

CHAPTER 2

NOELLE

I didn't just stumble back, I flew. "Excuse me?"

"You heard me."

"Is this a joke?" I aggressively asked. "Another one of your little games?"

"You used to like my little games."

"I used to like a lot of things that were bad for me."

He takes another step toward me. "We need to talk, Elle."

"Obviously, or why else would you be here?"

"I could think of a handful of reasons, and that's only referring to us."

I sneered a snide chuckle. "Us? There is no us."

"That's not how I remember it."

In one swift movement, he was in my face, catching me off guard. I faintly gasped when he was close to my mouth, only triggering all the times he caused this same response out of me.

He brushed the hair away from my face with the back of his fingers. "I didn't know you were the baker here."

Backing away from his fingers, I questioned, "And if you had?"

"I don't know..."

I slowly nodded, stepping sideways. It was now or never to make my voice heard. "I understand that you're technically my new boss, but I want to make something crystal clear to you, Nicholas."

His eyebrows pinched together as we continued to stare one another down.

"I've spent years proving to your grandfather that I could run this place without having someone manage me. I've sacrificed a lot of my personal life for this shop and this town, so don't think for one second that you're going to be the boss of me."

He held his hands out in front of him. "I know how you feel."

"Do you? Because from where I'm standing, you look content as ever."

"I'm not the enemy here, Elle."

"Really?" I mocked. "I don't know about you, but I sure as hell don't know how to see you as anything other than my ex-best friend, who turned his back on me without a second glance."

"I know you may think that, but it's not the truth."

"You don't know anything."

"I know that you're as pissed as I am right now."

"Could've fooled me."

"Trust me," he stressed. "I am."

"Trust you?" I exclaimed. "Now those are fighting words, Nicholas Saint Clair."

In the sincerest tone, he expressed, "I am truly sorry."

"Save those lies for someone who cares."

"At one point, you did."

"I was young and naive and didn't know any better. You

were the first boy to ever pay attention to me. It was easy to fall for all your lies."

"They weren't lies."

I beg to differ…

NICHOLAS

I couldn't help myself. Not with the way I left things. I never wanted to hurt her, at least not like that. Noelle was the only girl who ever meant something to me. Granted, we were young back then, but even now, having her this close to me for the first time in what felt like an eternity, it was as if no time had passed between us.

The spark.

Our instant connection.

It was still there.

Despite her pretending it wasn't, she couldn't fool me. Not for one second.

Reading my mind like I knew she would, she acknowledged, "You have no right to say that to me."

"I have all the right in the world to tell you how I feel. You wanted the truth, so here it is."

Her chest rose and fell with each word I confessed. "You always knew how to say the right things."

The door opening behind us wasn't enough to break our connection. Neither one of us moved.

"Good." Mr. Perkins walked in.

He was my grandfather's right-hand man. His voice echoed off the windows and walls. "You're not wasting any time getting reacquainted."

I peered over my shoulder. "We need another minute."

He nodded, grinning like a fool, and left.

My eyes met hers once again. "I hate that it has to be like this between us. Tell me what I can do to make this better."

"Nothing you can do will make this better between us. You betrayed me."

"Come on, give me some credit," I tried to reason. "That's not what happened."

"This is a nightmare," she snapped, shaking her head at me. "You'll say anything to get what you want."

"Well…" I smiled before I spoke from experience, "You know what they say—your best dreams and your worst nightmares usually have the same people in them."

We stood there for a few seconds. My inquisitive regard didn't falter. Although her eyes didn't move from my face, I still felt her stare on every inch of my body. So much so that she was the first to look away.

Bowing her head for a moment, she swept a strand of her hair behind her ear, trying to break the tension between us.

Unable to remain silent any longer, she questioned, "Where do we start with our tour?"

She never expected me to reply, "How about in my bed?"

Her mouth dropped open, and I laughed. "Oh, Elle, you should have seen your face! You're still too easy to tease."

My grandfather once told me that the Saint Clair men teased their women, and I never forgot that. I'd often catch myself doing it without even realizing it with Noelle. *I guess old habits die hard.* Our friendship was the only thing that made me happy as a kid. From that first day we met in the library, I was enamored with her.

She was easy to talk to, and everything came naturally between us. Our dynamic always bordered on best friends with casual flirting with a side of sexual tension and the possibility of mixed emotions. I'd be lying if I said I didn't like her. I did. I liked her a lot, and that hadn't changed, which wasn't surprising to me in the least.

Elle had this ability to take me out of myself. She always saw the good in me no matter what. Growing up, I was the prodigal grandchild and rebelled because of it. My entire family was obsessed with everything and anything related to Christmas. It had been that way since before I was born. Something about my great ancestors being traced back to Saint Nicholas, hence my name. Hopefully, this made you understand the legacy I had to live up to.

Except I had always been different...

Bah fucking humbug.

Where my family loved Christmas, I hated it—always had, always would. From the gaudy trees to the over-the-top decorations and the traditions everyone clung to like they were sacred.

Particularly my family.

Now, I'm stuck running this Christmas-possessed town with an avalanche of memories I spent thirteen years trying to forget.

But it wasn't just the town I abandoned... it was her too.

So I spoke the truth. "Elle, I asked you to come with me."

"Only because you knew I'd never say yes."

I shook my head, confused. "Do you hear yourself right now? You make no sense whatsoever."

She put her hands on her hips. "Oh really?"

I held my hands out at my sides. "What are we, ten now?"

Ignoring my remark, she continued, "You know how much I love this town. You knew I'd never agree to leave with you. You only asked me to clear your conscience while you ran away from everyone who loves you for no reason other than trying to prove a point to yourself that you didn't have to!"

"Elle," I coaxed. "That's not fair."

"What's not fair is that you own this place now! That's not fair! Do you have any idea how badly that sucks for everyone? Especially the town residents who have been here since before you were born. Everyone knows you hate it here! We live in fear that you'll immediately sell it off to the highest bidder without giving a shit about what they want to do with this place."

I scoffed. "And you think I could do that to everyone?"

She shrugged. "I don't know you anymore, and I more than likely never did."

"Noelle, you're the only one who did know me. I know you believe me."

"Again, with the right words, but your actions speak way louder. You can rest your case, Nicholas. Now, if we can get back to our tour, follow me this way, Mr. Saint Clair. I'll lead you to the kitchen."

She turned, about to take a step, and I grabbed her wrist, holding her in place. "Give me a chance to make things right between us. Please…"

She glanced down at my hold before looking up at me through her long, dark lashes. "Why now? Huh? Where have you been for the past thirteen years? You're only here because you have to be, and I refuse to be a commodity to you." She yanked her arm away. "I'm done with this conversation."

I watched her walk toward the back of the bakery and followed her, admiring the view. Even in her oversized overalls, she was still the most beautiful woman I'd ever seen. It was like the girl next door turned into a goddess. Her mid-length, wavy, caramel-colored hair bounced off her slender back, simply accentuating her ass that was perfectly molded against the jean material on her silky skin.

The familiar scent of her coconut shampoo mixed with her vanilla perfume had my head slightly spinning with each step I took. For the longest time, the smell of her lingered on my pillow well after I left. We used to watch movies in my bed for hours at a time. Our bedrooms were our hangouts growing up, and I recalled those warm memories often.

Maybe it was why I kept myself working. It was easier to forget the life I left behind. Especially the life I could have had…

With her.

CHAPTER 3

NOELLE

Later that night, I finished adding the final touches to my Christmas tree when my doorbell rang. Seconds later, Felix called out, "It's just me!"

I smiled, hearing his voice. "I'm in the living room!" I stepped off the ladder as his footsteps came down the hall, spinning to face him.

"Hey, you—"

He smiled big and bright, immediately holding up what looked like a cockapoo puppy in his hands. He was fully aware I'd never be able to resist such a fluff ball.

"Oh…" I held my hand out in front of me. "No, you don't!"

"Noelle…" he charmed, holding the adorable puppy out in front of him.

Wiggling my finger as if it would do something, I warned, "Don't you even dare, Felix."

"It's only for a few days. A couple of weeks, tops! Well, I mean… at least until he's old enough to be adopted."

"Felix… I have no time to take care of a puppy."

He held the fluff ball up to his cheek. "But look at him," he baited, unable to resist. "How can you say no to this face?"

As if on cue, the puppy stuck out his tongue, and I swear it shot right to my heart.

"I can't believe you're doing this to me right now. You know how busy I'll be until the new year."

"Doll, what's your excuse for the rest of the year?"

"Ha ha."

"Fine." He pouted the most pitiful face, and the cockapoo must have been a paid actor because he gave me those puppy eyes, and I was a goner.

Felix didn't miss a beat, adding, "I guess he'll just have to live at the shelter all by himself with no one to love him. Then he'll have abandonment issues and won't take kindly to strangers trying to adopt him. You know what happens when they don't get adopted, Noelle…"

I shook my head, bemused, "You Saint Clair men… the ability you have to get what you want is truly a remarkable talent that should be studied."

He smiled wide, knowing he got me.

Oh! Did I fail to mention that Felix is Nicholas's older brother by about two years?

What can I say? We became close after Nicholas left, but I had always been friends with them both. That said, I was Nicholas's girl back then, and I didn't know if that made any sense.

They also had a younger sister, Holly. She was five years younger than me, and they both lived in town. Felix ran the five-star hotel in the town square and helped with the animal shelter, while Holly ran the hair salon that stayed booked four months out. Every business in Mistletoe Town thrived; we made sure of it.

In three strides, Felix stood in front of me, and I was assaulted with the addicting puppy scent.

"Do you want to say hello to your new mommy?" He handed me what appeared to be a boy.

I reluctantly folded as if I was nothing more than a house of cards. "Temporary mommy, right?" The puppy fit into the palms of my hands, and I held his button nose up to my face to boop it with a kiss. "Oh my God! Why are you the cutest thing ever?"

The puppy licked my face in approval, already making me fall head over heels in love with him.

"On that note." Felix abruptly turned, obviously trying to get the hell out of there before I changed my mind. He swiftly hauled ass toward my front door. "My work here is done."

On his way out, I noticed all the puppy supplies he brought sitting by the foyer table.

Once he realized where my gaze went, he called me out, "I knew you wouldn't say no."

I rolled my eyes, kissing the puppy's head as I followed Felix out the door. It was freezing outside, but luckily, I was wearing my warm gingerbread pajamas with my matching fuzzy robe and house slippers. I was literally dressed head to toe in ginger-bread cookies and wouldn't have it any other way. The amount of Christmas clothes I owned was probably obscene, but again, I didn't give a shit.

They made me happy, and that was all that mattered to me.

While we stood at the end of my long driveway, Felix leaned in to kiss my cheek. "You just can't say no to me, doll."

I giggled, ready to tease him back, but a rough familiar voice roared from behind me, "What the fuck?"

I spun around, meeting Nicholas's stunned stare. "What are you doing here?" I snapped, annoyed to see his mug for the second time that day in only a few short hours.

Nicholas completely ignored me, gesturing to Felix. "What the hell are you doing here with her?"

"Excuse me," I argued, bringing Nicholas's attention over to me. "That's none of your business. What, are you stalking me now?"

Nicholas signaled to my house. "You live here?"

"Yeah." I nodded. "This is my home. Now, why are you—"

The instant grin on his face was enough to cut me off. "Meet your new neighbor."

As soon as the last word left his lips, my mouth dropped open, and it felt like he just dumped a bucket of ice-cold water on top of my head. It was horrible.

"You're renting the Buller house?"

Nicholas smiled. "It appears so."

"Ugh," I sneered, beyond frustrated with how my life kept shifting in every direction as if Ebenezer himself had taken the wheel. "Why wouldn't you stay at your parents' hotel?"

Without letting him reply, Felix answered for him, "Because Mr. Big Shot thinks he's better than us, that's why."

"That's utter bullshit," Nicholas defended. "And you know it."

"Then why haven't you visited all these years? Why didn't you come to Grandfather's funeral? We all know you're only here because you have to be, so let's not beat around the bush and call a spade a spade, shall we?"

"Listen, you condescending dick. You think this is easy for me? I'm the first person to agree with you that I don't deserve Mistletoe Town, and quite frankly, I don't want it."

Felix shook his head in disappointment. "That's a damn shame."

"You need to stay out of this."

"Stay out of what exactly? The fact that Noelle can't stand you?"

Nicholas winced, and for some reason, his reaction pulled at my heartstrings.

"I know, little brother. The truth hurts, right?" Staring him directly in the eyes, Felix kissed my cheek again, and I could've sworn I heard Nicholas growl from behind me.

At that moment, there was no denying my lingering feelings toward my ex-best friend.

Now, only looking at me, Felix smiled. "I'll be back to check on you two tomorrow, and I'll fix your fence for *our* new baby."

Nicholas scoffed, "Baby?"

I chuckled a little at his dismay before I lifted the puppy in the air. "The furry kind."

His eyebrows pinched together. "You bought a puppy with my brother?"

Felix didn't hesitate to piss him off. "And what if we did?"

CHAPTER 4

"Okay..." I stepped between them, breaking up whatever pissing contest this was over me.

They did this growing up too. They always had some sibling rivalry over the dumbest things. I think it had a lot to do with Nicholas being the favorite grandson despite his hate for such a special holiday and sacred town to all of us.

"I'll see you tomorrow, Felix."

With his stare focused on his brother, Felix reluctantly nodded, stepping back as he made his way toward his car. At the last second, he added, "I'll clean up your driveway and fix your garbage disposal too."

"You're the best," I thanked him.

In one final punch to the gut, Felix antagonized, "I guess I'll be seeing you tomorrow morning then, right, good ole Saint Nick? Or is the prodigal son not going to grace us with his honorable presence?"

"I'll be there with bells on," Nicholas mocked.

"Hmm... that'll be the day," I mumbled under my breath while Felix gave the puppy one last ear rub and left.

These two had always been like night and day. Nicholas wasn't like any of his family members. He was actually the opposite. He and Felix were constantly bumping heads, and I knew it wholeheartedly hurt Felix that their grandfather chose to leave this town to a man who technically turned his back on everyone in it.

Especially his family.

I didn't bother to turn around. Instead, I started making my way back inside when Nicholas suddenly asked, "Why does my brother have a key to your house?"

I abruptly turned, standing strong. "So what if he does? What are you going to do about it? Come to think of it, you don't get to do anything but stand there and wallow in your own cold Grinch heart and Scrooge soul."

His hand dramatically flew to his heart as he made a grunting sound. "I know you didn't just offend me looking like the gingerbread woman?"

I chuckled, choking it back down immediately. Before he could see he was getting to me, I opened my front door, and he yelled out, "I always preferred your holiday onesies!"

I smiled, hating myself for it until I finally closed the door, safe and sound inside. His reminder provoked the exact response he desired. I thought about all the times I paraded around him wearing very tight spandex little numbers that I didn't think twice about. It was how our friendship was, and neither one of us had an issue with it.

"This isn't over, Elle!" he exclaimed through the wood as if he knew what I was thinking. "You can't hide from me! I'm your neighbor now! Besides, can't break tradition! Where's my Mistletoe Town welcome basket? Huh? I don't see my cookies!"

"Cookies are only for good boys," I whispered to my new puppy as I made my way into the kitchen.

After I had situated and organized my new life with a baby, Nicholas caught my attention through the big window as I walked toward the stairs. He was rolling his luggage up his new driveway with a bewildered expression.

"Why does every house have to look like Santa took a shit on it with Christmas lights and candy canes?"

I bit back a laugh.

Every house but his…

If he thought he would win this between us, he had another thing coming. Since he demanded Mrs. Claus hospitality, I'd have to deliver whether I wanted to or not.

The last thing I wanted to do was not treat him like another tourist wanting to experience the winter wonderland that was Mistletoe Town. The second the thought struck me, it started to snow, and I took in the beauty of the white flakes cascading down the frigid night sky.

I was about to walk up the stairs to my bedroom when I heard him yell, "I fucking hate snow!"

For the rest of the night, I tried not to sneak a look at him through my bedroom window. His bedroom window was right next to mine, and all the windows paralleled one another for both homes. The main reason I had drapes was to ensure my privacy everywhere I walked in my house.

The Bullers' home, on the other hand, had been vacant for a while, and they only just got furniture delivered last week. They were still awaiting window treatments for their renters. I owned my two-story, three-bedroom, two-bath, twenty-five-hundred-square-foot house with a pool. This was the second thing I bought after my car a couple of years ago. I loved everything about my home. There wasn't anything that wasn't designed to meet my style.

It was my pride and joy, and I took the best care of it. It was everything you'd picture a cozy baker's sanctuary to be. It felt like a home from the moment you stepped into the open foyer with a huge snowflake chandelier above your head. It was only one of the endless amounts of decorations I had displayed for this time of year.

If I was being completely honest, I kept up with some of it year-round, like the gingerbread cookies. To say I had Christmas decor coming out of my ass was an understatement. Not only was my attic filled with decorations but my garage and basement were too. I had to buy an extra storage shed in my backyard to hold even more decorations, but I'd yet to build it.

I made a mental note to book a handyperson through that referral service I used for a cleaning crew. I needed someone to help me set it up. I had no idea how or where to begin assembling something that large. I always felt terrible asking Felix to help me with honey-do lists around my house, but he was insistent I do. He never let me pay him, which made matters worse. I mean, we casually flirted sometimes, but it was harmless fun. He wasn't my boyfriend, and we'd never gone on a date, so there was no reason for him to do those things for me.

Taking the puppy out to potty one last time before bed, I laid him in his crate, and he whined instantly. Nothing I did would make him stop crying. I hated that I had to do this, but he needed to be crate trained, or I at least had to try. By the time three thirty in the morning rolled around, I got an unexpected text from an unknown caller.

Throwing the silk pillow off my head, I grabbed my phone off the nightstand. Blinking away the haze and darkness, I slowly read the words on the screen.

For the love of God... can you please make that tiny terrorist shut the hell up?

· · ·

Nicholas?

Noelle: How did you get my number?

Nicholas: It's funny how numbers work. It's the same one you've always had.

Noelle: Considering you never used it after you left, I figured you forgot it, but it wasn't until you changed your number that I got the real message.

The bubbles kept appearing on and off my screen, indicating he was writing and then deleting what he was trying to text back until another message dinged through.

Nicholas: Clocks.

Noelle: Clocks? What does that mean?

Nicholas: Put a clock in the fluffy dictator's crate. It's supposed to mimic their mother's heartbeat.

I hated listening to him, but I didn't have much of a choice if I wanted to get any sleep. First, it took me a second to find a clock. Thankfully, I had one in the guest bedroom. I placed it near his face, and he immediately leaned against my hand like he didn't want me to leave.

I was a sucker, lying down where I was so he could snuggle against me. He was still technically in his crate, and I called that a win. Little by little, the tiny dude calmed down, and I texted Nicholas again.

. . .

Noelle: Better, your highness?
  Nicholas: Indeed, my queen.

Now, there was no hiding or fighting it this time.

I smiled…

CHAPTER 5

NICHOLAS

I didn't know what I hated more, the fact that everyone who walked through those custom, gold-lattice, iron doors that were bent to look like it was a Christmas tree early the following morning was bright-eyed and bushy-tailed or the fact that I had to be there. What made matters worse was that everyone kept congratulating me as if I'd won the grand prize when it couldn't have been further from the truth.

At least it was for me.

"Oh my God!" Mrs. Sanders fawned over me, grabbing my face to blow air kisses in my direction. "Look at you!"

She was the sweetest woman and my old man's secretary for the past thirty years. She was basically part of the family at this point. It was her outfit that caught my attention the most. She was decked out in a head-to-toe Christmas tree outfit, including the gaudy jewelry hanging off her skin.

I wish I could tell you she was the only one dressed like that, but I'd be lying. Out of the ten people in the room—including my brother and father, who were both board members—I was the only one dressed in a pair of jeans and a button-down, sporting a beanie.

It was fucking freezing outside. The temperature had dropped overnight since it started snowing. I lived in a warmer climate now, and I didn't own clothes thick enough to handle this frigid weather anymore. Plus, I never really cared for this weather. Most of the board members were dressed in some sort of Christmas apparel, whether a tie, a vest, or some socks. You'd think the dress code was holiday attire.

I guess the more things changed, the more they stayed the same.

Everything about this town was still the same, from the decorations to the displays and lights. I was almost certain you could see Mistletoe Town from space, bright and beaming off the globe from the holiday light shows. There was practically a snowman on every corner and a nutcracker soldier not far behind it.

I'd only been awake for two hours, and I'd already seen Santa Claus twice. He was the best Santa lookalike that money could buy, and the board spared no expense to find the most authentic staff for The North Pole, located at the end of town. It was the big finish to this place. A five-story wood log cabin that was decked out to look like Santa's workshop to include pictures with the mystical myth himself, along with the one and only scam artist, his wife, Mrs. Claus. The elves and whoever the hell else added to the cast of Christmas cheer bullshit were most certainly in that building.

Beside it was an ice-skating ring. I used to play hockey in school, and during my senior year, I was the team captain. I lived there while growing up, yet I hadn't stepped foot in a ring since I left. Something I used to have a passion for turned into an afterthought I only had when I saw a postcard or a movie that involved the sport I once loved.

I couldn't help but remember all the memories I had trying to teach Noelle how to skate. She had more interest in playing in the snow than skating on it. However, she did love snowboarding, which was a hell of a lot easier for her to learn. She was good on a board, and I wondered if she still enjoyed it as much as she did back then.

Her love for all the seventy-foot Christmas trees through town captivated her the most every year. Each tree had a specific theme. My personal favorite was The Grinch tree near the library. I smiled when I walked by it that morning. Another thing about this supposed magical place was that you could walk everywhere and anywhere. Very few used their vehicles. Most went by foot or bikes. It was one of the things that made this place so safe from crime and car accidents.

The speed limit through the entire town was restricted to twenty-five miles per hour. However, that was due to all the tourists who would drive their cars through the town to see the lights and displays that were skeptical among the gingerbread houses. There was even a sled driven by the impostor himself and his real-life reindeers, including the star of the show, Rudolph. Of course, you couldn't forget the train for the Polar Express.

You could literally hear children's laughter from the sleds and tubing at the Candyland shop, or you could book a ride on a horse and carriage to take through Winter fucking Wonderland. In theory, this place was someone's paradise and dream come true, but in my reality, it was my own personal hell and worst nightmare that I now owned.

From the time I understood it was all smoke and mirrors, there wasn't a time I thought Santa was real. Noelle used to say it was my origin story, due to my older cousins spilling the truth without realizing I was there. I knew the truth from the start, and I thanked them for it. Someone had to keep their sanity in a town filled with Christmas cheer twenty-four seven.

If you asked me, I was the Grinch, and I had no problem owning up to it. If anything, I aspire to be left alone. My nickname growing up used to be Grinchy, and I dressed like my misjudged hero every year for Halloween as a kid. I even had a dog named Max who looked like Grinch's companion. He passed away when I was sixteen, and to this day, I still thought about him. Now I didn't have time for a dog.

The only time I was home was to sleep or shower. If I wasn't at my office, I was on a jobsite meeting with clients, roofers, the county and so on and so on. The list of bullshit I had to deal with on the daily was enough to drive any man to drink. Luckily, I never cared for the stuff. Being a carpenter was what I enjoyed the most about my career. I subbed out the rest, yet I still had to deal with managing the project, which was the hardest part of the contract.

My shop was a thirty-five-hundred-square-foot warehouse that held my entire life under the aluminum. I had a stage area along with an area I could work. Since I never took time off, my clients all understood I needed to walk off the job for a few days, and I was able to sneak away until after Christmas.

I sat back against the doorframe and leaned against it after my father and I had an awkward greeting. He barely looked my way, making it obvious he was not pleased with my grandfather's decision either.

"Welcome, Nicholas," a board member by the name of Phil greeted, tearing me away from my thoughts.

In the blink of an eye, we were all sitting at a long rectangular table while I sipped on some hot coffee, trying to warm up. I wasn't much for sleeping and got by very little, or else I'd be hurting this morning from the tiny terrorist who decided to whine for most of the night.

"We can't tell you how excited we are to finally have you back here in Mistletoe Town with us."

I smiled, nodding at Mrs. McQueen. She was the town treasurer.

"I've given everyone a brief overview of who you are even though most of us already know," Mrs. Henderson, the chair of the board, announced. "But I figure it'd be best for us to discuss all the details in person and with everyone present."

I could tell by the expression on their faces they were hesitant about where this was leading.

"There are only a couple of things you need to immediately handle," she continued. "But first, rest assured that your grandfather handpicked our entire team, and each person brings their own level of expertise to whatever they're responsible for. We all promised your grandfather that we'd make sure our T's are crossed and our I's are dotted. Do you understand?"

My hands were tied at the moment, and I had no choice but to listen. It almost felt like I was sitting in a room full of adults treating me with kid gloves.

I hesitantly nodded, unable to say much.

She proceeded with her pitch. "People love to feel like they're a part of something, and given the fact you're the CEO, you're the biggest face of the town. So bottom line: low risk, high reward. Mistletoe Town makes a lot of money and provides for many families who live here themselves. We pride ourselves in hiring our own."

"Yes," Mrs. McQueen agreed, smiling wide. "Truly learning the ins and outs of how this town runs will help you excel in your new role. Being the grandson of your late great grandfather means you have some huge feet to step in. There's a reason that towns like this don't exist, and we want to keep it that way."

"All that sounds great"—Felix snubbed his nose where it didn't belong—"but we all know it doesn't mean a damn thing to him. He couldn't care less about the glorified title."

I was about to open my mouth to respond to my dickhead of

a brother when the double doors that were designed to look like Santa's suit, including the belt, opened. I jerked back…

Suddenly caught off guard when Noelle walked in.

CHAPTER 6

NICHOLAS

W ithout taking a look around, she merely declared, "Good morning, Mr. Saint Clair."

I arched an eyebrow, confused about where she was going with this. I didn't want to play these little games with her. Once sitting in the black leather chair, she leaned forward with her elbows on the table.

She nodded, her composure steady and unwavering, but it didn't matter how poised she appeared while sitting there staring at me. I knew what was beneath her ridiculous elf dress.

"Nicholas, this is—"

"I know who Noelle is, Mrs. McQueen."

"Oh… I apologize. I wasn't aware you knew who she was."

Noelle didn't show any emotion over my presence or response. She was too busy portraying a woman who didn't care for me, and that was the hardest pill to swallow. I thought after our text last night I may have made some leeway, but I was dead wrong.

She was not swayed in the least.

Coldly replying, Elle bit, "I'd prefer you address me as Miss Woods."

Narrowing my gaze at her, I countered, "Why do I have to call my best friend Miss Woods?"

"I'm not your best friend, and I don't want to beat around the bush. I'm only here because I run the publication and the press committee in this town you turned your back on, and we're all concerned about your image."

"My image?" I shot back.

"Yes." She firmly nodded. "Your anti-Christmas persona doesn't exactly speak highly for itself, and there will be media, news stations, and journalists from all over the world until Christmas is over. This time of year, the town is swarmed by press, and you know it."

"And why is that my problem?"

"It should come as no surprise to you how influential you are right now to Mistletoe Town."

"So, I'm influential to everyone except to you?"

She glared at me. "Can you please stop airing our private business to everyone in the room?"

"You're the one who came in here like Elf on a Shelf, guns blazing. I have no interest in performing for the public or be whatever spokesperson you all expect me to be."

"Nicholas..." my father warned in a voice I didn't appreciate. "It's a necessary evil, and it's what's best for the town."

I didn't allow another second of this ambush. Instead, I simply ordered in a sharp tone, "We need to clear the room. I'd like to talk to Miss Woods alone."

"I don't think that's the bes—"

"Whose name is on those documents?" I interrupted my brother, and he cleared his throat before nodding for everyone to leave.

After they were gone and the door was shut behind him, I

crossed my arms over my chest and focused solely on the woman who thought she could change me.

Again.

"Now that they're gone, let's cut the bullshit, Elle."

"Mr. Saint Clair, I won't remind you again to address me as Miss Woods."

"How long do you plan on playing this cat and mouse?"

She stood abruptly, sliding the documents across the table as she spun, strutting her way to the door. "Take a look at the holiday itinerary for the next few days leading up to Christmas because I control you beginning tomorrow morning."

I resisted the urge to argue, realizing all too quickly that it seemed like I'd be dealing with her the most.

"If that means I only have to deal with you, I'll gladly take the bait."

HR would have a field day if they knew I was admiring her luscious ass that swayed with each step she took. It felt like forever had passed, waiting for her to walk by me. Too many emotions and questions tore through my mind in those brief seconds, one right after the other.

The clicking sound of her heeled knee-high boots vibrated deep within my core the closer she got toward me. One by one, it added to all the chaos erupting in my mind.

My throbbing head meant a migraine was looming, and I was surprised I could still see straight with the uncertainty racing through my body. All I wanted to do was pull her into my arms and have her stop with the games she was trying to play. The wall she built against me; I worried I might lose this battle between us.

When she walked past me, I growled at my impulsive thoughts and grabbed her hand, tugging her back toward me. She instantly misplaced her footing and fell into my lap, catching herself on my chest while her knee flew right to my balls.

I loudly groaned as spots instantly danced around my eyes.

"Oh shit!" she exclaimed, jumping off me. "I'm going to get you some ice!"

I wanted to reply, but I couldn't. Words couldn't form out of my mouth when I felt like my balls were in my throat. From the moment she dropped to her knees in front of me, setting the freezing ice on my balls, I envisioned this scenario happening in a much different way.

"Hell of a defense tactic."

She leaned back, sitting on the heels of her boots. "Are you alright?"

"I'm not sure yet."

"Do you want me to take a look?"

"You want to look at my balls?"

"No, but I would if you were hurt."

"Would you kiss them to make them feel better too?"

She bit back a grin, trying to pretend my teasing didn't affect her.

I didn't know what I was expecting.

What I wanted from her.

I liked having her here. With me. Just not in this town.

Her scent.

Her hair.

Her soft skin.

It all did something to me in the same way it used to.

Unable to revert, I spoke the truth, "You can play this game all you want, but we both know it's only a matter of time until you're dealing with us."

She pushed off my knees, standing tall in front of me. "In your dreams. Me kneeing you in the balls doesn't change our relationship, Nicholas."

"But look what it's done for your perception. You're saying we're in a relationship now."

"Don't twist my words, or this will be a very long day."

"It will be if you continue this charade of not giving a shit about me."

"I don't know what you expect from me."

"I'd love for you to give me a chance to make things right between us."

"Which includes what?"

"How about we start with dinner at my house?"

"I don't want to have dinner with you."

"Dessert then? Breakfast? Shit, I'd settle for coffee."

"Not happening."

I smiled, eyeing her up and down, and I didn't hesitate to remind her. "As you know, Elle, I never back down from a challenge, so consider this war, Miss Woods."

And I meant every word.

CHAPTER 7

NOELLE: THEN

My dad was away for the weekend, and I was used to staying alone—military life.

"Cute candy-cane onesie," Nicholas expressed, walking into my living room as I grabbed a blanket from the back of my couch.

We were going to watch a movie.

My cheeks flushed, and my belly fluttered. If there was one thing I learned about Nicholas since I met him a few weeks ago, it was that he spoke his mind anytime he opened his mouth. He never held back, and in the little time we knew each other, it was one of the things I liked the most about him. He seemed as genuine as they come.

It was refreshing.

He was my breath of fresh air.

Which was yet another reason I liked being around him.

I smiled. "I thought all guys—"

"Do me a favor, Elle. Don't think about other guys when you're with me."

I rolled my eyes, but I still found myself smiling.

"Are you a Leo?"

He nodded.

"That makes so much sense."

"What are you?"

"A Libra."

"I don't know much about signs."

"Well, we're complete opposites; however, we line up the best in the zodiac signs for any kind of relationship. You're the yin to my yang and vice versa."

He chuckled. "Grumpy, sunshine?"

"Something like that."

He was a relentless tease. His eyes bore into mine and once again rendered me speechless. He stared at me with that same swagger and confidence he exuded all the time. Another thing I liked about him was how he looked at me.

There was something about him since the first time I laid my eyes on him that I couldn't tear my gaze away from. This magnetic pull I was instantly drawn to.

It came from something deeper.

More meaningful.

A connection I couldn't explain grew stronger with each minute passed between us. I knew he felt it; he was the type of guy who would notice everything. Neither of us said a word for a few seconds, but it didn't matter. Our eyes spoke volumes, causing the nervous feeling in my core to subside.

"Tell me some more about yourself, Elle."

"What do you want to know?"

"Everything."

"You say that like you mean it."

"I don't say anything I don't mean."

I ignored his response, asking, "What do you want to know?"

"I mean, you don't have to tell me your blood type or

anything, but I do want to know if you're a psycho, and I need to be worried that I'm in your house. Especially because your house looks like Santa took a shit on it with Christmas lights."

"I'm not a psycho. I just love Christmas."

He flopped onto the couch in front of mine. "And what's so great about it?"

I shrugged. "What's not great about it?"

He shrugged back. "Where do you want me to start? How about with the fact that we're just supposed to believe some man can travel all over the world in one night, breaking into people's homes? In what universe does that make sense because, in this one, that would get you arrested."

I smiled. "I didn't say it was logical."

"So…" He paused for effect. "You're admitting it's all one big lie we tell children to con them into being nice to stay off the naughty list. This is simply a disciplinary tactic adults use and is used far too much if you ask me. Honestly, I don't see how kids aren't scared of the jolly old fat man. To me, he's scarier than Freddy, and that lunatic can get you in your dreams."

"You are seriously comparing Santa Claus to Freddy Krueger?"

"They're on the same playing field. I mean, they're both after children."

My mouth fell open. "That's horrible."

"You're telling me. I've been saying that shit forever."

"I'm saying you're horrible."

"I know…" He leaned back into the couch. "I'm too honest. I'm sorry to burst your bubble if you thought I'd be different. I don't believe in the mayhem that this holiday creates for every-one. It's all about presents and decorations and traditions, ugh… it makes me exhausted just thinking about it. The stress and pressure parents put on themselves to create core memories and magical experiences could cause high blood pressure alone, and we both know what that leads to. I bet they hide all the medical records proving it does."

"Who hides them?"

With a cheeky expression, he winked. "If I told you, I'd have to kill you."

"And you're worried I'm the psycho?"

He grinned.

"Why would they hide them?"

"To keep the masses spending money."

"Hmm..."

"Makes sense, right?"

"Yeah, from a realist perspective. I'm an idealist."

"You know what they say, opposites attract."

Feeling ballsy, I blurted, "Does that mean you find me attractive?"

"I'd be blind if I didn't find you attractive, Noelle, and even then, I'd sense that you were beautiful."

I blushed.

"The red in your cheeks matches nicely with the candy canes on your onesie."

We locked eyes. "Well, besides that." I changed the subject. "You really are the Grinch."

He grinned again. "I've committed to it my entire life."

"I see. So you've never been in a relationship? Never had a girlfriend?"

"And that surprises you, why?"

"I don't know. Your family seems like they have their shit together."

"I guess as much as a family can with putting immense pressure on their son to be someone he doesn't want to be."

"Hmm..."

"Are you judging me now? I'll never lie to you, Elle."

"You're implying that you'll see me again? I thought you didn't do relationships?"

"I don't count making you smile as a relationship."

I giggled. "How you can go from making me sad that you hate my most favorite time of year to making me laugh is beyond me."

"What can I say?" He smiled. "It's a gift."

"You're a paradox of contradictions, Nicholas."

"Do you need to start slow?" he coaxed, bringing it back around to me. "How about I lead you in the right direction? Tell me your favorite color?"

"I like anything bright."

"Like your eyes?"

"No, like your eyes."

I smiled again as he took me in with that smoldering stare. Knowing he could see right through me made my stomach flutter for entirely different reasons. Despite the awareness in his eyes, I looked away. I had to. Reaching into my purse, I turned my attention to a tiny candy cane I was pulling out, avoiding the look in his eyes. I put it in my mouth, needing some sort of distraction from the sudden realness between us.

The cool peppermint chilled my lips, calming me down a little.

"I could see you as the little boy who terrorized kids with your spiel…"

"And you would have enjoyed it then as much as you are right now."

As if on cue, my stomach did that somersault thing. Except this time, it felt like it would never end, twisting and turning and flipping.

Never taking his eyes off mine, he leaned over with a mischievous glare, and I felt this jolt. This immediate spark that made my mouth dry and my face flush, a burning sensation all over my body. I had never experienced anything like it before, yet I couldn't wait to feel it again.

He cocked his head to the side as if he knew exactly what I

was feeling, thinking, wanting. He moved to sit next to me when I put on the movie. His hand was always on my thigh, brushing his fingers ever so lightly over my sensitive skin.

We laughed.

We joked.

We picked on one another.

The night rolled by, and it was like I blinked, and the sun was peeking in through the sliding door that stayed open all night.

We didn't sleep.

I was never bored.

I couldn't remember the last time I had this much fun by simply speaking to him. Doing something completely out of the ordinary for me and enjoying every second of it. This night meant more to me than it should.

He reminded me of the girl I was supposed to be, to act my age, and live in the moment with him.

The moment would be over soon…

"Wow. I can't believe we talked all night."

He nodded, stretching like a lion beside me on the couch. "It's a first for me too."

We were both laying our heads on the arms of the sofa with our bodies beside each other. We stayed like that all night. He never tried to put the moves on me. All he did was snuggle next to me under the blanket, and that was that. It felt more personal, though, just hanging out and getting to know one another.

"Your parents aren't—"

"They're at a gala for the weekend. The only one who needs to be babysat is my little sister, Holly. She's cute but a pain in the ass."

"And your brother?"

"He's a bigger pain in the ass. He's probably at his girl-friend's. He spends most of his time with her anyway." He stood, cracking his neck. "I should go."

I followed him as he walked to the front door with the blanket wrapped around my body. I was always cold, and I noticed he ran hot. We were definitely living up to being opposites.

Do we kiss? Say goodbye? What happens now?

Question after question tore through my mind until we arrived at the entrance. I turned the lock, opening it, but it abruptly shut from behind me, making my eyes shift to his over my shoulder. My eyes widened, and my belly did a somersault times ten.

"I … umm … I—"

He pulled me into a tight hug and kissed the top of my head, muttering, "I'm glad you moved here."

"Me too."

Pulling away first, he added, "I'm going to be at the rink later today if you want me."

"Yeah." That was the only word I could form.

Is this a date?

It was only then that I understood it didn't matter.

For some reason, his friendship meant more.

CHAPTER 8

NICHOLAS: NOW

I walked into my friend Dan's exam room. He was now working at the hospital in Mistletoe Town. He was a doctor on his residency and recently moved there with his wife and their new baby. They wanted to build their life there like most new families did. I built a deck for the hospital he used to work at during his medical school time a few years back, and we'd been friends ever since.

He knew I grew up there and the history with my family. It took him a minute to believe I was the grandson of such a prestigious legacy, and I didn't blame him. I tried to stay out of any press since I understood who we were. I wanted to live my own life, and I didn't want people from all over the world to know who I was before they even met me.

I wasn't a fan of being the center of attention. I was the kind of guy who stood in the back and observed the crowd, and once I felt comfortable, I'd loosen up. Maybe it was the Leo in me, always in control. Dan was also aware of my inherited holiday and how I felt about it. He was a good friend, and I never thought I'd be seeking his advice in this town of all places.

At that point, I had to talk to someone, and I figured he'd be the one who would understand me the best—being a neutral party and all.

"Look at you," I greeted. "You're all dressed up in your doctor clothes."

"They're my scrubs, you dick." He didn't beat around the bush. "How did it go with the best friend?"

"Not good."

"That memorable, huh?"

"You could say that."

"You going to see her again?"

"Yeah," I replied, quickly adding, "she's the town baker."

"Oh, shit…" His eyes widened. "Huh, how did I not put two and two together until now? Damn. She makes the best choco-late chip cookies. Did you know that? Have you eaten her cookies?"

"Trust me, I wish I could tell you I've eaten that cookie."

"Damn."

"Let me rephrase; as a teenager, it wasn't like that with us. I mean, of course, I always found her attractive and we got along great, but that doesn't make for a relationship, you know?"

"Actually," he exclaimed. "I don't know because to me, that's exactly what starts a relationship."

"No, that's a friendship."

"I think you are wrong, but you were saying…"

"As a man, our friendship and connection are still there, but what's changed is my desire to eat her cookies."

"I see…"

"I've never felt such a physical reaction to a woman before. It's surreal, and I honestly don't know how the hell to deal with it, let alone where we go from here."

"Now I know you're messing with me. You never had sex?"

57

I shook my head.

"What?"

"What part of that did you not understand?"

"The whole thing." He stood there with a stunned expression. "What do you mean you never had sex?"

"We never had sex," I repeated.

"Why not?"

"I just told you it wasn't like that."

"For you?"

"For both of us."

"Because of you?"

"What are you getting at?"

He leaned against the exam table, folding his arms over his chest. "You have commitment issues."

I jerked back, never expecting his response. "That's not true."

"How do you figure it's not? Why else would you run away from paradise? This town is amazing. You were set up to thrive without even having to prove yourself."

"Maybe to have my own life," I reasoned, needing someone to understand why I had to leave. "Maybe so that I wouldn't live in a place where buildings are named after my entire family, and everyone kisses my ass for it."

"Yeah," he snapped. "Look at what good that did you? Now you own it."

"No shit, and the only thing I got for it this morning was a knee to my balls."

"Wait, what?"

"Noelle."

"She kneed you in the balls?"

"Yeah."

"What did you do?"

"I pulled her toward me."

"Wow." He smiled. "She's violent. I like it."

"No." I chuckled. "It was an accident."

He wiggled his eyebrows. "So she says…"

"Let's just say it didn't go according to plan or how I imagined it would."

"I don't understand."

"Here I thought you'd be the one who would understand."

"Me? Why me?"

"I don't know. You're married and have a kid."

"And that makes me mature enough to understand women? Especially your relationship with your ex-best friend who you're still obviously madly in love with?"

I didn't just jerk back, I stumbled. "I'm not in love with her. I mean, I do love her, like her, I'm just…"

He beamed. "In love with her."

"Fuck you, man. I like her."

"You like a lot of things."

"No, I mean—*I really like her.* I like her so much that I can't imagine my life without her again."

"Hell has officially frozen over!" He put his hand up to his ear. "Excuse me? I'm sorry. What was that? Can you say that one more time? I don't think I heard you the first time."

"You heard me, dickwad."

"Oh, come on, this is a monumental moment. A universal standstill. The Grinch is flying all around us. Now admit that you're in love with her and secretly love Santa, and we'll call it a day."

"I came here for advice, and this is what I get from you?"

"You're right. We should take you to the ER instead. You need a radiologist to x-ray your head on the fact that you're pussy-whipped, and you haven't even seen hers yet."

"Fuck you again."

"You like her? Like, you want to date her and see where it goes, or you like her and want to be besties again?"

"Besties?"

"That's what all the cool kids are saying these days."

"Because it's important to sound like them?"

"Bet."

My eyebrows pinched together. "Bet what?"

"Your balls because Noelle already has them."

I laughed. "You're an asshole."

"Bet."

"Bet what?"

"It means yes, Mr. Saint Clair, master of Mistletoe Town."

I turned to leave. There was only so much bullshit I could take, and my cup had run over that day.

"Chill… I'm the last person to be giving you advice."

"Obviously." I halted my departure, shifting my eyes back to his. "Yet I'm still here."

"Aw, hell… can't take a joke now, Grinchy? Man up. Does she know how you feel?"

I shrugged. "We kissed a few times in high school, but it was mostly under mistletoes. It was kind of our thing…"

"You're more pussy-whipped than I thought," Dan remarked, annoying me further. "Don't women have a sixth sense about this stuff? She can probably smell it on you, but if you don't want to go the route of being honest with her, then I suggest you just go with it for her. You like her, show her. Simple as that."

I inhaled a deep breath, contemplating what to say next. In the end, I decided to change the subject. "What about the town? I still don't want it, and I have to do all these festivities beginning tomorrow. You should see the itinerary. It's ridiculous. I'm going to have tinsel coming out of my ass by the time this is over."

"When what's over?"

"Christmas."

He scoffed out, patting my back. "I hate to break it to you, Mr. Saint Clair, but there is no over for you. You own Mistletoe Town, remember? Get used to it."

I thought about it for a second before I answered, "The only saving grace is that Noelle will be my babysitter."

"Then I'd use it to your advantage."

"What do you mean?"

"If you want her to forgive you, then you need to show her that you've changed."

"In what way?"

"In all of it."

"But I haven't."

"Then you should."

"That makes no sense."

"How much do you want the girl? You ask a woman like her out for one reason and one reason only. Do I have to spell it out for you? Girls catch feelings quick, so I'd make sure you understand what you're doing when it comes to her before you string her along."

"What's that supposed to mean?"

"It means maybe you're ready to settle down and have a girlfriend. Or maybe you're just lonely."

"I'm not lonely. There's just something about her. There's always been something about her."

"Always?" he asked, glaring at me like a deer in headlights. "You mean you've been thinking about her all these years?"

"Maybe."

"How often?"

"Often enough."

"Why didn't you call her?"

"What are you, Dr. Freud?"

"Well, Sigmund would tell you it stems back to your mother, and come to think of it, that makes sense." He nodded. "You're screwed."

I pointed at him. "You know what? This conversation hasn't helped me in the least. If anything, you've made me more confused."

"Well, pull up those panties and start acting like the man she needs if you want to get her back in your life. You said she's obsessed with Christmas. I'd start there, my friend."

"You can't be serious."

"As a heart attack."

"That's the shittiest advice you've ever given me. I feel personally offended by what you just suggested." I shoulder-checked him and walked toward the door.

The audacity of him to tell me to pretend to be another one of my worst nightmares.

I wouldn't turn into Saint Nicholas.

I refused to.

CHAPTER 9

NICHOLAS

From the moment I walked into my rental house, the lyrics for "You're a Mean One, Mr. Grinch" played through the speakers, and I was slapped in the face with nothing I could have ever expected.

"You've got to be fucking kidding me?"

Cujo cockapoo came barreling down the hall, wearing one antler in the middle of his head and a red reindeer nose. He resembled Max from *How the Grinch Stole Christmas*. It didn't end there; it was only the beginning. The entire entrance was decorated in Grinch decor.

"Oh my God..." I strained through a clenched jaw. "I'm going to kill her..."

Cujo barked, quickly detouring to the left, and I was slapped in the face yet again with the twelve-foot, fully decked-out Grinch Christmas tree in the back of the open space of the living room. I wasn't talking about a few ornaments thrown on a tree.

No... there was a whole ass Grinch head where the star or

angel should be, and his arm hung out the side with his signature pinched fingers, holding a string that had a red glittery ball dangling from it.

The rest was themed out the same way with ornaments and several huge Whoville-type bows while ribbons and garland shined bright with all the mixed patterns surrounded by warm colored lights.

To top it all off, it had plush dolls of Cindy Lou, Max, and the Grinch hanging off several branches. These weren't decorations you could buy in one shopping spree; this was years and years of collections, and I didn't have to wonder where it all came from.

I was upset she didn't ask my permission, fully aware I'd say no. However, the thought and time behind this was too much for me to ignore. At least it was themed out to my liking, but I'd never repeat it out loud.

Especially to her.

The last thing I wanted to do was give her false hope that I turned into the man I always dreaded.

I couldn't help but shift my gaze from one decoration to the next, from the obnoxious couch pillows to the Whoville blanket and everything in between. There wasn't a character she didn't bring into this house. Including the entire town of Whoville in ceramic glass, which was displayed by the big front window. Despite the house looking like the Grinch literally moved in, it was somewhat tastefully done, whatever that meant.

Before I could utter a word, Noelle appeared out of thin air. "Surprise!" she shouted from behind me, walking into the room with trouble in her arms disguised as Max.

She wore a sweater that read "Mrs. Claus working for the Grinch" proudly displayed across her chest. The Santa hat, skirt, and knee-high red boots with matching stockings really brought the whole outfit together for me. The Santa hat was a nice touch.

"I'm surprised you only did the inside." That was the first thing I could muster when she was wearing something like that.

As a kid, I used to appreciate her little outfits, but now, now, it was on another level of how much she fascinated me and kept my attention. I dated some through the years, but it was never serious. My business was my priority, and I didn't leave room for much more.

"I'm doing that tomorrow," she sassed, aware I knew she meant it.

She took off Max's 2.0 headpiece and put him in his crate that was suddenly in my living room as if he had moved in as well.

Once Noelle was looking at me, I gestured to the open space. "Is this your idea of a peace offering?"

"No," she confidently baited. "This is my grenade."

"Well, what do you know?" I mocked. "I caught it, and now I'm holding the pin. The way I see it, you have two choices. You can surrender to me, or I'll have to punish you for being a bad girl."

"Surrender to you? What the hell does that mean?"

"It means you owe me a dinner."

She extended out her hip in a defiant manner. "A dinner for what exactly?"

Twirling my index finger in a circle in the air beside me, I responded, "Need I say more?"

"Oh," she celebrated with a pleased expression on her face. "I'm getting punished for bringing some holiday cheer into your life? Also, do you need me to remind you that you specifically asked for the Mistletoe welcome, and I'd hate not to live up to your town expectations." She left for a minute and came back with a cookie basket. "That reminds me, I made these for you."

I wasn't going to pass up one of her delicious cookies. Reaching into the basket, I grabbed one and immediately took a big bite. Within seconds, I was spitting it out into my hand.

"Oh yeah…" she mocked in a snide tone. "I ran out of chocolate chips, so I used raisins instead."

Wiping my mouth with the back of my hand, I walked into the nearest bathroom and tossed it in the trash where it belonged.

"You know how much I hate raisins," I called out, stepping back into the room.

"Oh yeah…" She smiled wide. "Oops."

"This is how you treat your new boss?"

"I'm just following your orders and trying to make you feel welcome."

"Is that a threat?"

She winked at me. "Never."

"Does that mean you won't have dinner with me?"

"That's exactly what it means."

Listening carefully, I asked, "You're choosing to be punished, then?"

In two determined strides, she was in my face. "Mrs. Claus never backs down from a challenge."

I grinned, knowing I just won the golden ticket. Without thinking twice about it, I followed Dan's advice to show her I really had changed.

Specifically, when it came to *her*.

Gripping the back of her neck, I tugged her toward me.

In a steady breath, I warned, "Then I'll have no choice but to bring out the Grinch in me."

NOELLE

My hands were pressed against the mantel on the brick fireplace beside the tree in one quick movement. The heat from the flames instantly warmed my skin as he spread my legs from behind.

With my back now to his front, it gave him the leverage he sought.

What is happening?

My mind raced with mixed emotions while my body completely betrayed me. It didn't just melt into his touch—it molded.

Shit!

I needed to stop this.

I couldn't let this go any further.

Why can't I get my mouth to move?

"You feel that fire?" he asked into my ear in a husky tone that wasn't referring to the flames burning in front of us.

There was a mirror in front of us, and I caught a glimpse of our skin glistening in the fire's soft glow as the song changed to "Santa Baby."

He rubbed his lips against the soft skin of my neck, rasping, "Now you're on the naughty list..."

NICHOLAS

Her heated gaze lingered on the Christmas ribbon I was pulling off the tree. Slowly, I draped it around her waist.

"I like to wrap my gifts before I open them."

Instead of tying her waist, I tied her wrists, and she didn't stop me. If anything, the brazen glimmer in her eyes indicated she wanted me to keep going.

I didn't struggle with my conflicting emotions at that moment. I thought I'd be trying to decipher between right and wrong, but the lines were blurred for most of our relationship, and by the expression on her pretty face, it was a mutual thought.

After hanging her wrists on a strong nail, holding up a heavy stocking, I brought her pouty lips to mine, and she sucked in a breath.

"But if you're a good girl... maybe I'll even let you come down Santa's pole."

She giggled in that addicting way. "You're horrible."

It wasn't our flirty banter that was anything new between us, it was my actions following through with what I was saying that was new. I slowly began to slide my fingers up her inner thigh.

"Don't you want a white Christmas? Because I could stuff your chimney, seeing as my stocking is so well hung." I smiled. "Don't you want to fill the Grinch with your holiday spirit?"

Smiling as she leaned her head against my chest, she questioned, "How many puns do you have?"

"Elle…" Inch by inch, I made my way up her leg. "We both know I can go all night with burying my face in your mistletoe."

Her eyes glazed over, dilating.

It was all the encouragement I needed to slide my fingers over her silk bottoms and her pussy.

"You're really pretty when you're wet, Elle."

She sucked in another breath, shutting her eyes and leaning farther into me, almost like her legs were buckling. "You're definitely on the naughty list," she panted.

"I thought we settled this the first day we met. I'm eternally on the naughty list, babe."

"You remember that?"

"I remember everything."

I was barely touching her through the thin satin on my callused fingers and her clit, but she was already breathless for me. Slowly, once again, I continued my sweet torture, back and forth, a little faster each time, driving her to the brink of insanity.

The way she breathed.

The way her mouth parted and her tongue moved to wet her dry lips.

The way her body responded with every movement of my hand until all of a sudden, she drew in a rigid breath against my lips as soon as I spanked her ass…

Hard.

Causing her to stick her ass out farther at the angle I wanted, and her wrists struggled against the ribbon.

"You've been a bad girl, Miss Woods... what would Santa say?"

Not faltering, she snapped, "To go fuc—"

I spanked her ass again. "I'm sorry, what was that? To go what?"

She glared at me, and I grabbed the vibrating Santa hat off the mantel beside her wrists before I placed it on her clit. She hissed upon contact, making my cock twitch from the moan that quickly followed.

"What were you saying? Huh? You want me to go what?"

It didn't take long for her knees to buckle and her eyes to shut.

"Ah..." Her body quivered, pulling at the ties still knotted around her wrists. "You're not playing fair."

"You think I care?"

She was coming apart at the seams, and I loved every second of it.

"What do you say?" I teased. "You want to cum for me?"

Her mouth opened as I intensified the pressure of the Santa hat against her clit. Her pussy was getting wetter, only betraying her torn stare as she started to come.

Her chest heaved, and her pussy surrendered.

She wanted me to kiss her.

She wanted me to touch her.

She wanted me to claim her.

I didn't.

My stare instantly caught her dark, hooded glare, fighting the urge to give her what she wanted. Our eyes caught in the mirror, and we watched each other for a few seconds before that was enough to drive her over the edge, making her come down my hand.

She was warm.

So fucking warm.
And I was fucked…

So royally fucked.

CHAPTER 10

NICHOLAS: THEN

"Nicholas, where are we going?" Noelle asked, tugging on my hand to slow down.

I always forgot how wide my stride was compared to hers. She'd been trying to get me to answer for what felt like the hundredth time in a matter of minutes. It was evident early on my girl had no patience. It was her first anniversary of moving to Mistletoe Town, and I wanted to do something nice for her. I didn't give it too much thought. I just did what came natural to me like I always did when it came to her.

It was just what best friends did for each other.

As she followed me close, I continued walking through the woods, carefully stepping in my tracks. Mother Nature chose that morning to unleash her wintery fury, practically shutting down the whole town in the process. The ground was covered in frost, blanketed by a dusting of snow, while huge, soft flakes fell from the sky. The frozen fluff crunched under our boots, and with each step, we treaded deeper into the forest. I held her hand tighter so she wouldn't slip on the fallen branches coated with a thin layer of ice.

I checked on the surprise I'd been working on in the woods earlier that day, making sure it was still good to go.

"Come on." I nodded toward the faint glow of lights in the distance. "We're almost there."

I started walking on the uneven ground again, tugging her behind me. I spent all my money from working jobs over the past couple of months. Between hockey and school, I didn't have much time to work on side jobs throughout the town, but now that I got a truck <u>for</u> my sixteenth birthday, I'd be able to take on more work on the weekends. I didn't want to rely on my parents. I never did.

They did get me my truck, and I was grateful for it none-theless. They ended up ruining the sentiment after they reminded me that I was Nicholas Saint Clair and needed to start working for one of their businesses. I could be making more money with them than I was with my handyman work. It wasn't about the money, though. It never was, yet they didn't understand that. They didn't even try to understand me.

I tried not to focus on any of that, wanting to make this day special for Noelle. We finally approached a small clearing where the snow continued to rise beneath our feet. The look on her face the second she saw that I'd turned part of the woods into a winter wonderland was the only gift I needed that Christmas.

"Nicholas, I can't believe you did this," she whispered, completely caught off guard.

Her eyes shifted from all the colorful lights strung around the trees to the makeshift Christmas trees surrounding us that I decorated. I themed it using her favorite gingerbread house and bright colors in the lights and decor. It was the life-size ginger-bread house I built with my own two hands that really knocked her on her ass. The painting and design took me the most time, but the actual carpentry and build only took me a few days.

I watched her walk around the open space, grazing her bare fingers along the wood with a smile across her face. She twirled around as the snow fell down on us.

"I can't believe you did this for me."

I shrugged it off like it wasn't a big deal. "I had some free time."

"This is the sweetest and kindest thing anyone has ever done for me. Truly."

Her eyes rimmed with happy tears when she looked deep into my gaze.

They say the smallest decisions could change your life forever. I'd always remember this moment for the rest of my life.

I told her to look up.

She did.

Right there above our heads was the blue mistletoe I hung.

"You don't see the blue one that often." She stated what I was thinking when I bought it.

I nodded, waiting for I don't know what.

A signal?

A sign?

I wasn't really sure.

When you're sixteen, how much do you really know?

This kiss would hold me over until I could do it again every year. I didn't intend to start this tradition between us, but I guess you could say this was where it began for us.

I kissed her under the mistletoe every year, knowing how special that was.

This would become the only tradition I ever cared for. I wish I could describe the intensity I felt with her at that moment. Only I couldn't do it justice. I couldn't put into words what felt so right.

I leaned in and kissed her.

Her lips parted a bit, and I opened mine too. However, it was over before it even began.

A tree branch breaking broke our trancelike state, and we pulled away from one another. Her hair was a mess of waves, she smelled like cinnamon, and it was doing all sorts of things to my head.

How the hell did she smell this good all the time?

Neither one of us said a word about what just happened. Instead, we completely blew it off. For the next hour, we ate the snacks I left in the picnic basket earlier that day in the gingerbread house. We sat on an extra-soft blanket I spent way too much time trying to find. Christmas lights were all around us, and as much as I hated to admit it, it was magical.

Like Hallmark.

Stuff you'd seen in a holiday rom-com movie.

Even with that, I didn't give a shit.

I ate it like my cold holiday heart had grown three inches.

I watched the way her lips moved with each giggle that left her mouth.

I watched the way her body leaned into mine with each second that passed.

I watched the way I made her smile.

Laugh.

Blush.

"You're a great guy. You know that, right?"

"Verdict's still out on me," I remarked.

She was glowing.

Radiant.

Bright, shining, stunning.

"Why are you looking at me like that?"

"How am I looking at you?"

"Like you've never seen a girl before."

"Not one like you."

She blushed again.

"You're a relentless flirt. You know that too, right?"

I grinned. "Only with you."

"You always know the right things to say."

"Well, you bring out the best in me."

"Is that so?"

"It most certainly is."

"You know my mom warmed me about boys like you."

Despite Noelle's mom passing away unexpectedly, I liked that she always talked about her. It was almost like it made her feel closer to her or something. I enjoyed hearing their stories. It was obvious she was a good mom. She kind of reminded me of my own.

"Want to see the best view in the town?" I asked, standing and then reaching down for her.

"Of course." She grabbed my hand, and I easily lifted her.

"You afraid of heights?"

"No. Why, is it not safe?"

"For the most part."

"Nic—"

"I'm joking. You'll be fine, I promise."

We hiked up the hill for the next thirty minutes until her nervousness subsided, and she saw the view ahead. You could see the entire town from up there, and it looked exactly as if it were a winter wonderland postcard in real life. I watched her take it in for the first time as if I was experiencing it that way even though it was probably one of my favorite spots.

I went there often, especially when I needed to think. It was a great place to be alone. Not many people knew about it, and I wanted to keep it that way. It felt like our town always belonged to random tourists coming in and out.

She grabbed my arm, leaning her head against my shoulder, and we stayed there for a long time in silence. No words were needed between us.

It was already written in the sky and Christmas lights.

CHAPTER 11

NOELLE: NOW

After I tended to the puppy I still hadn't named, I placed him back in his crate, and he went right to sleep. He seemed to feel more at home in Nicholas's house, which I noticed immediately when he made himself at home as if he wanted to live there instead.

In one breath, Nicholas professed, "I hope one day you can find it in your heart to forgive me. If I could go back, just know... I'd do things differently."

I tried to find my bearings as he untied the ribbon around my wrists, having to move away from him. Now it was my turn to stay silent, not knowing what to say or how to say it.

To my surprise, he broke the silence between us, adding, "For the first time in my life, I'm contemplating if I went in the right direction."

"Because of your inheritance?"

"Because of you."

I swallowed hard, listening to every word he was openly sharing. Nicholas always spoke his mind, but this was still new and different. We never talked about our feelings in this way. Despite the number of mistletoe kisses we shared, it didn't change our friendship for one second.

If anything, we grew closer, but in our friendship.

"What I love about fixing and building homes is I don't have to be anything for anyone."

I didn't make a sound.

"I did what came naturally to me, and I knew it was the only way I'd ever get out from under my father's thumb. I wanted to prove to him that I didn't need him like everyone in this town does. That I could stand on my own without his money, his influence, and all of the important people he knows. It's why I lived and breathed my business since I left here, Elle. It was never personal. I swear it."

"But you still left me and now you're back and not only are you the owner of the town I love, you're also technically my new boss. Do you have any idea how hard that is for me? Did you ever stop to think about me for one second?"

"I was a kid," he stressed. "Come on, cut me some slack. If I had been in the mindset I am now, I would never have done that. The last thing I wanted was for you to feel like you or our friendship never mattered to me."

Standing my ground, I explained, "You're acting like nothing's changed when everything has, and now we've added whatever the fuck we just did into the mix."

"I hate to break it to you, but we've always added whatever the fuck we just did into the mix, Noelle."

"This was far beyond kissing, Nicholas."

"So now you're complaining?"

"I'm confused."

"Let me unconfuse you." I grabbed her shoulders. "I like you, Elle. I've always liked you."

"What does that even mean?"

"It means exactly what I just said. I like you more than a best friend likes their best friend, and I always have. I was just too young and stupid to identify what it was back then. I thought I had to make something of myself. I thought it was the only thing that mattered."

"So what? I was holding you back?"

"This town was."

"I'm a part of this town."

"No shit. It's why I stopped calling you. You were still here, and I hated it had to be that way. Especially when I asked you to leave with me. I was hurt you said no, okay? Despite what you think, I never thought you wouldn't leave with me."

"I don't believe you."

"Why would I lie about that?"

"I don't know..." I shook my head, inhaling a deep breath. "It's just hard for me to think you thought I'd turn my back on this place."

"I guess I underestimated your love for a home I hated."

"You don't hate it here; you just like to pretend you do."

"Noelle—"

"If you hated it here as much as you claim, you would have never made my yearly anniversary a special day since we met."

"That was for you."

"Not true. Every year, you added some sort of decoration to our secret spot in the woods, and we'd go up the mountain to see the town in all its glory. I've seen your face. I know what you experienced when you were there with me."

"Whatever you have to tell yourself."

"That's such a Grinch thing to say."

"Well, it's all I got. So here I am, asking you, no, actually begging you to give me a chance to make things right between us, and I'm not talking about me making you come. That can stay on the menu all the time. Whether you love me or hate me, I can make you come as many times as you please. I have no problem making you come morning, noon, and night if you want me to."

I bit back a smile.

Damn him.

"But the friendship part. The best friend part." He gestured between us. "Let me make that right again. I was young and made a mistake, and I promise I won't do that again."

"How do you expect me to trust you?"

I didn't hesitate in replying, "Let me earn it."

I wanted to believe that what he said was true with everything inside me. However, nothing could have prepared me for this moment and the emotions it would evoke.

It was evident that our connection was as strong as ever. I wanted to hate him, be mad at him, resist him.

Except I was definitely late on the resisting him part, and I'd be lying if I said the sexual tension hadn't been building for years before he left. The older we got, the worse it became.

In four long strides, he closed the distance between us with so much force that my body slammed against the wall behind me. I hit it with a hard thud.

Instantly, Nicholas caged me in with his arms, making me feel his sorrow and remorse.

And his hate…

Not for me.

For himself.

CHAPTER 12

NOELLE

"I mean it, Elle. I'm so fucking sorry."

I replied in the only way I could, I crashed my lips onto his, and it was all he needed to lose control. Roughly, he gripped my ass, lifting me to straddle his waist.

Our kiss was passionate.

Hungry.

Sending us into a frenzy.

I didn't realize he was walking us into his bedroom until he laid me on the bed, spreading my legs to lay between them before he lowered himself onto my heated body.

This was crazy, but Nicholas and I were always impulsive. Going from one extreme to the next. This wasn't unusual for us other than not being able to keep our hands off each other. The only opinions that mattered about our relationship was ours, and it seemed as if that hadn't changed either.

I craved to give him what felt like it'd been his the entire time we were growing up. And who was I kidding? It wasn't like I dated much in the past thirteen years, so maybe it had been his then too.

In this current place and time, it seemed as though this man, my ex-best friend, owned my heart.

My heart.

Body.

Soul?

He cradled my face, never once breaking our intense kiss. Something was different about him as he hovered above me. He kissed me deeply as his hands ran down my shoulders to hike up my sweater.

"Nicholas," I rasped, trembling beneath him, and he was barely even touching me.

I had no idea what I was in for.

"Let me help you out of that ugly sweater."

"Hey!" I chuckled. "It's vintage!"

With a wicked grin, he vowed, "I know the next gift I'm giving you tonight."

In the blink of a passionate eye, my clothes were gone, and I was left in nothing but my stockings and boots…

And Santa hat.

Once I was naked and completely exposed, he deliberately took his time taking in my body. My thighs clenched together when I felt his stare heading toward my core. I could feel my wetness pooling between my legs from his touch.

Fueling my need to feel him.

Anywhere and everywhere.

All at once.

He elicited a moan from my lips when I felt his hand slowly expose my clit.

"Can I take a picture of your pussy so I can show Santa what I want for Christmas?"

I smirked. "I thought you didn't believe in him?"

"Your body makes me more excited than anything I've ever

had under my tree." Holding my thighs, he scooted his way down to the floor and dropped to his knees. "How about we forget the next couple of days of your bullshit Christmas itinerary, and you just give me a couple of days of you instead?"

Before I could reply, he buried his face between my legs, making my back jolt off the bed, which earned me a chuckle as he moved his head up and down, side to side, using his tongue to manipulate my pussy like it was made for him.

Don't get me wrong, I'd had guys go down on me, but I always faked it. I just gave up hope that men knew what they were doing when visiting the area. That was kind of how it felt —they were passing through and didn't want to commit to a location.

Now Nicholas…

He wasn't simply committing to a location; he was becoming the fucking mayor in a matter of seconds. Maybe it was from still being overstimulated from his impromptu sex toy escapade where I'd never be able to look at a Santa hat the same.

It didn't take long until I was panting.

And moaning.

And of course, begging as he continued with his oral assault.

He never stopped working me over with his lips and tongue when he started to slide his finger into my warm, wet heat.

"Oh God…" I moaned, curving my back into the mattress beneath me. Coming undone from his touch.

He devoured me with his tongue and fingers, making love to me with his mouth. Sucking harder and more demanding with each passing second, to the point I thought I was going to pass the hell out.

A loud, rumbling growl escaped from deep within his chest. He was losing control, which made me surrender to his power over me.

I came.

I came so hard I saw stars, and still, he didn't let up, making me come over and over again.

Against his mouth.

His fingers.

His tongue.

I started to convulse, my body moving of its own accord, and he instantly locked his arm around my lower torso, keeping me in place.

My back arched off the bed, my hands white-knuckled the sheets, and my body shook with so much force that I thought I would never stop coming down his chin.

"Oh God ... ahhh..." I profusely panted, my body turning on me.

Orgasm after orgasm.

They were coming quick and fast, one right after the other.

"Please... Nicholas ... please..." I squirmed, begging him to stop, tugging hard at his red hair to the point I thought I was going to rip it out.

His beard between my legs wasn't something I expected to enjoy as much as I was. He released my clit with an unrelenting groan, not wanting to stop but allowing me mercy. Thrusting his tongue into my heat, he licked, ate, and swallowed up all my juices, and I swear it was the hottest thing I'd ever seen or personally experienced.

He sat up with a pleased and satisfied expression on his face, grinning as he wiped his lips and chin with the back of his arm. Showing me precisely how much of a mess I made.

And in true Nicholas smart-ass Saint Clair fashion, he teased...

"Looks like Santa isn't the only one coming to town..."

CHAPTER 13

NICHOLAS

"For fuck's sake," I grumbled, breaking into Noelle's house so easily.

I barely maneuvered the lock and walked right in. I placed my tools on the table and made my way to the kitchen. She was being difficult, saying she didn't want to have breakfast with me. She claimed she had a meeting with a family for a hundred-person Christmas party coming up.

I didn't expect her to welcome me with open arms after what happened last night, but I figured I'd at least get to bring her some coffee. Once I saw her jump into her SUV at nine in the morning, I got right down to business, knowing I had my work cut out for me. If she thought she could get rid of me that easily, she was in for one hell of a rude awakening.

I wasn't going anywhere but back into her life where I belonged.

For the rest of the morning and by midafternoon, I was finishing up with why I was there in the first place. Grabbing a cold beer from her fridge, I made myself at home since she had no problem breaking into my house the day before. I was simply returning the favor.

I heard the front door open, but that wasn't what surprised me. What shocked the shit out of me was that she walked in holding pepper spray in her hands.

"What the hell, Elle?"

She jumped, turning in the direction of my voice, her Mace now pointing at me. "Oh my God! I could have maced you, you idiot! What the hell are you doing here?"

"Put the Mace down," I ordered.

"Not until you tell me what you're doing in my house uninvited."

I was over to her in three strides, grabbing the Mace out of her hands before she even saw it coming.

"What are you doing with this?" I asked, placing it on her coffee table and turning to face her.

"Why does one carry Mace, Nicholas?" she sarcastically stated, pissed off that I was able to take it away from her without any effort. "I thought you were a robber. My door was unlocked."

"And what is a hundred and fifteen pounds of you going to do?"

"Mace him!" she exclaimed with her hands out in front of her. "Hence, the Mace!"

I gripped the back of her neck and pulled her toward my mouth as her pupils dilated and her breathing hitched, not giving her a chance to think about it.

Not.

One.

Second.

My lips were on hers before she had a chance to blink. My hands clutched the sides of her face as my tongue devoured her perfect pouty lips, biting her bottom lip.

Her soft tongue.

Her peppermint scent.

The taste of vanilla in her mouth.

It had me groaning involuntarily.

She moaned into my mouth, making my cock twitch.

When I knew I had her where I wanted her, I pulled away, but not before demanding, "Let's role-play, and you play nice and stop acting so naughty unless you want the Grinch to steal your Christmas."

With that, I let her go and made my way back into her living room to grab my tools.

NOELLE

Damn him.

My body felt like it was on fire. There wasn't an inch of me that didn't ache for him, that didn't want him. I craved his touch now as much as I did last night, and my cocky ex-best friend knew it too. I licked my lips, needing the moisture to soothe the burn he left behind.

His eyes followed the simple gesture of my tongue.

His desire overwhelmed me, but him being in my home with his tools intrigued me too much not to ask, "What are you doing here?"

He replied, "I came over to tackle your honey-do list. My brother doesn't need to be your bitch now that I'm back."

"You're back?" I snapped. "What does that mean?"

He ignored my question, walking toward my front door instead. Only then did it register what he did all day for free without me having to ask him. I didn't actually have a list. He must have literally examined my house to search for what needed fixing.

After he left without saying another word to me, I ended up making my way through my own home to see what he'd been up to. I couldn't believe he tackled a list that was probably a mile long in just a couple of hours. Including the shed that had to be built.

It was done.

Everything was fixed or built, and he even laid a couple of carved stone rocks that were too heavy for me to lift into my garden for me.

Thankfully, I could leave the puppy with Felix for a few hours while I rushed home to prepare for the annual Christmas parade that began the holiday festivities. I didn't have time to contemplate anything else as I stepped out of the shower, wrapping the towel around my body as I walked toward the kitchen.

There in all his clean glory was Nicholas again, leaning against the wall with one leg over the other. Once again, he was devouring me with his eyes.

Bastard.

He looked sexy as sin, and that was exactly what he was…

My own personal hell.

"You need to go," I ordered, my resolve breaking as I took in every sexy inch of him.

He grinned, a mischievous gaze quickly replacing the heated one as if he could read my thoughts. I swallowed the saliva that had suddenly pooled in my mouth. My skin felt flush all over, and he wasn't even touching me. He pushed off the wall, and for a second, I thought he was coming toward me. Instead, he made his way into my kitchen, opened the fridge, and grabbed a cold beer.

Unbelievable.

He twisted the cap off and placed it on my counter, not even bothering to throw it away. After taking a few sips from the bottle, he made this low, exaggerated groan from deep within his chest. Normally, this scenario would have turned me on. He looked good in my kitchen.

The intensity that radiated off his demeanor had me weak in the knees, and I found it hard to breathe. He slowly licked his lips with his predatory stare as he eyed me up and down, and I knew what ran through his mind.

I should have moved.

I should have run.

But my feet were glued to the floor.

I couldn't move them, even if I wanted to.

And the sad part was…

I didn't want to.

I wanted to believe his reasoning on why he stopped keeping in touch with me. I swear I did, but I couldn't yet because it didn't take away the hurt I held on to for all these years.

Before I knew it, he stood in front of me. Pulling my hair away from my face, he grazed his knuckles against my cheek. I closed my eyes and allowed myself to lean into his embrace.

Into his comfort.

Into his touch.

Into his words.

"I'm here to take you to the Christmas parade."

I hated hurting him.

I wasn't that kind of person.

My eyes shot open. "What?"

"You heard me."

"And then when it's over and we're walking back to our houses, I want you to bring over the rude cockapoo for a sleepover."

"Nicholas…"

"Come on," he countered. "You used to love our sleepovers."

"Yeah, because we slept. I have a feeling that won't be the case this time around."

He grinned. "I can keep my hands to myself… now, my mouth? That wants to taste you again. I woke up wanting to eat you for breakfast, and since you decided to deny me, I fixed your house instead," he explained in a low tone, dripping with seduction.

"Thank you."

He smiled. "My pleasure. Now try to deny you don't like me in your home. I dare you."

"You're not playing fair."

"I'm not playing at all."

"I'm putting my foot down."

He laughed, a husky and throaty sound escaping from his mouth. "Your foot doesn't even make noise when you stomp it."

"I can't—"

"Can't or won't?" He interrupted.

"I... I don't know."

"Yes, you do."

"I wish it were that easy. I wish I could close my eyes and pretend I can forgive you, but I'm not entirely sure I can yet. I need you to understand that."

He sighed deeply, the frustration evident.

"At the end of the day, nothing has changed. I still live in Mistletoe Town. This is my home. I don't even know where you live. I don't even know how long you'll be here. I don't know anything, and quite frankly, neither do you because, at the end of the day, you're only here because you have to be. We both know you wouldn't be here if you hadn't inherited this holiday."

I had no idea how we had come full circle. He had an effect on me like no other man ever had or came close to. He was definitely pulling out all the stops, and I'd be lying if I said it wasn't working.

I didn't give him a chance to reply. "Are you trying to buy my affection by pretending you want to go to this Christmas parade with me?"

"Depends." He smiled, trying to lighten the mood. "Is it working?"

It was pointless to argue with him, and I was beyond over it at that point. So I played the only card I had left...

"Fine. You want me to go with you, then you're going to have to do something for me."

"I like the sound of that."

Little did he know, he wouldn't like anything about the grenade I was about to throw.

Except this time…

I pulled out the pin before throwing it.

CHAPTER 14

NICHOLAS

She stepped toward me, not backing down. Not that I expected her to. "I don't want to go with you."

I cocked an eyebrow and folded my arms over my chest, her eyes traveling from my face to my body. "You never were a good liar. It's time you stop acting like I don't know you."

Clearly still choosing to be defiant, I could see in her eyes that she was up to something.

"Maybe you don't."

I chose my words carefully, lacing my tone with cockiness directed right at her. I took a step toward her, expecting her to move back.

She didn't.

"Is that right?" I replied arrogantly, centimeters from her lips. "I don't know you? Really? What part don't I know? Maybe I don't know the way you move your hair to cover the side of your face when you're nervous. Or maybe I don't know how you bite your bottom lip when you're deep into your baking. Or do you mean that I don't know the way you freak out if it's too dark in a room and you won't walk in? Or maybe I don't know that you bite your fingernails when you think no one is looking. Oh wait, here's a good one. I don't know that you're trembling in your skin right now. I don't know that your heart beats a million miles a minute, your hands are clammy, and you can't swallow. How hundreds of thoughts are going through your mind, but the top one being how bad you want me to kiss you. How badly you want me to fuck you. How bad you want me to claim every fucking inch of your perfect body." I paused to let my words sink in, and her flushed complexion gave away that everything I was saying was true.

"You're right. I don't know you. I don't see your gorgeous smile in my sleep. I don't hear that ridiculous giggle you have when I'm away from you. I don't see those dark brown eyes every time I close mine." I leaned in a little closer so she could feel my breath against her lips.

Her breathing hitched, and her eyes dilated. All it would take was for me to kiss her and bite that bottom lip that had me hard just staring at it.

I didn't.

I wanted her…

Needed her…

To come to me.

"I'm pretty sure I know you. I know exactly who you are."

She licked her lips, trying to conceal the smile from my examples that described her to a T.

"Any more doubts I can clear up for you, Elle?"

I swept her hair away from her face, and the mere touch of her cheek against my fingers restrained me from the impulse to back her up into the wall and remind her of who she belonged to.

Her resolve was breaking again. It was written all over her beautiful face. I never expected what happened next.

Not in a million years.

NOELLE

"Noelle, you gotta be messing with me," he let out, holding up a heap of red velvet that was suddenly on his chest. Cocking his head to the side, he stared at me with no trace of amusement in his bright green eyes.

I bit my lip so I wouldn't fall into a fit of giggles.

With the most believable serious expression I could muster, I cleared my throat and replied, "Oh, come on, it's for the kids, and it's not that bad. I even called in a few favors. You're wearing one of Santa's suits, so you could be the best Santa." Smiling wide, I gave him one hell of a smirk.

I couldn't help it. I burst out laughing.

"Oh... you think this is funny, do you?"

Straightening up, I once again cleared my throat. "No. I'm not laughing at you. I'm laughing with you."

"I'm not fucking laughing, Elle."

I choked back another chuckle. "I'm laughing for both of us. You may not think this is funny right now, but it's one of those situations you'll look back on later and think it was hilarious."

"Hilarious, my ass. What I do find funny is the fact"—he pointed a stiff finger at the suit lying beside me—"you think I'm actually going to wear that."

"This is the only way I'll go with you."

"Hate to break it to you, but the kids aren't going to believe I'm Santa."

"Maybe the older kids won't, but the younger ones will."

"This doesn't make me happy."

"Christmas Eve is in two days, and you know the kids will be so excited to see Santa in the crowd. Plus, it'll make me happy, and I guess I could be one of Santa's little helpers. Do you want me to dress up as Mrs. Claus?"

He bit out, "Then you'll just have to jingle my balls so I can give your pretty face a white Christmas."

NICHOLAS

This fucking suit.

I spent most of the night sweating my balls off while playing the part. All the while, I couldn't stop thinking about Noelle's tight, wet pussy coming on my face. So I willed my dirty mind to keep busy by interacting with a shitload of kids who were so happy Santa Claus showed up in the crowd. They took turns telling me what they wanted for Christmas.

By the end of the night, I was getting restless, checking the time every few minutes. I anxiously waited for the night to end with Noelle in my bed. I failed miserably at distracting myself from my throbbing cock, aching to be freed from these hot Santa pants.

It wouldn't be much longer now. The parade was winding down, and soon, the kids would all be tucked into their beds, which was exactly what I wanted with my Mrs. Claus.

She was dressed in a Mrs. Claus getup, and I couldn't keep my stare off her. I'd be lying if I said it didn't piss me off that she was basically the belle of the ball. The number of men who surrounded her at any point in time was like a kick to my balls. I wasn't the only guy fascinated by her, and I couldn't help but wonder how many of them had actually gotten a chance with her.

Which led to more questions about how many men she'd slept with…

"Look at you," Felix mocked, standing beside me while the parade flew by.

"Yeah," I confidently responded. "There's nothing I won't do for my girl."

He jerked back. "You're here with Noelle?"

"Yeah," I repeated. "We're on a date."

He narrowed his gaze at me. "Bullshit."

"She's sleeping in my bed tonight. And quite frankly, it's

none of your business, but since it's obvious you like her…" I stepped toward him, stopping when our faces were inches apart. "She rode my face last night." I smiled.

He scoffed, snapping back around. With his hands fisted at his sides, he left. I wouldn't normally kiss and tell, but someone needed to get him off his high horse, and I had no problem being the man who knocked his ass off.

"What was that about?" Noelle asked, walking toward me.

I ignored her question and asked my own. "You ready to go? I think I've been punished enough for the night."

"But look how happy you made everyone." She smirked. "Including all the press. The board will be happy you're taking your new role seriously."

"Dressed like Santa Claus, the irony."

She laughed. "Admit it, you had fun."

"Whatever you have to tell yourself."

I grabbed her hand, nodding above me, and she instantly looked up, realizing there was a mistletoe there.

Without thinking twice about it, I grabbed the back of her neck and kissed her as if we weren't in front of the whole town. I didn't want anyone to be mistaken about what was happening between us, especially since I needed to keep other dicks away.

Literally.

I pecked her one last time, leaning my forehead on hers as snow slowly started to fall on our heads.

"Now for the real question." I asked, "Do you want to sit on my lap and tell me what you want for Christmas?"

Her lips parted against mine, and she softly panted, "Tis the season…"

And I didn't waver. I spoke with conviction, "To fall for you."

CHAPTER 15

NICHOLAS

I chuckled, shaking my head, grabbing her by the waist and making her squeal when she tried to walk by me in my bedroom after changing in the bathroom.

"Did you think you could walk by me without me touching you? Especially when you're wearing that."

"It's a dress."

"It's a shirt you wear as a dress."

"I have a tiny torso."

"You have a tiny everything. That tight little pussy of yours could tempt a saint."

She turned to face me, cocking her head to the side and placing her hands on my chest. I leaned forward like I was going to kiss her, but at the last second, I clicked my teeth together like I was going to bite her.

"Are you trying to provoke me?"

"It depends. Is it working?"

"So you want to ride my sleigh tonight?"

She looked down at her watch. "I guess I could fit you in, but

Santa, is that a candy cane in your pocket, or are you just happy to see me?" She played coy.

We took the puppy for a walk, and it was almost midnight. I still hadn't changed out of my outfit.

"I don't know, Elle. Why don't you get on your knees and come find out, so you can empty Santa's sack?"

"But... it's not Christmas yet."

"Elle, unlike Santa, I come more than once a year."

She giggled, twirling a strand of her long hair, and it was still the sweetest sound I'd ever heard. Noelle knew exactly the role she wanted to play in this perverted Christmas fantasy.

"But what would the elves say?"

If anything, she taunted me with her long lashes.

Kissing down the side of her neck, I moved my fingers onto her bare inner thigh, making her moan in approval. My fingers skimmed higher and higher up her long, silky skin.

She sucked in a breath, anticipating my next move as I continued my gentle torture for a few more seconds. I inched closer and closer to where she wanted me to touch her the most.

"Stand up." She did, cocking her head to the side and backing away a bit.

"Take your dress off for me," I ordered, leaning on the back of my hands to enjoy the show that was Noelle Woods.

She reached for the hem.

"Slower."

She slowly lifted her dress over her creamy thighs, and I rubbed my fingers over my mouth, already tasting her on my tongue. She threw her dress on the floor and stood in front of me in nothing but her bra and panties.

"Turn for me."

She did.

"You're so beautiful," I murmured, loud enough for her to hear.

She reached for her bra and took that off too.

"Be careful, Santa, or Mrs. Claus may come down your chimney."

I grinned, pulling her to me. Within seconds, I was lying on top of her. I purposely trailed my callused fingers down the slit of her pussy.

"I prefer to give rather than receive. After all, I am Santa. I'm used to going all night." Lightly brushing my fingertips farther down her slit, I slowly slid her panties to the side. "Feels like Mrs. Claus is having a very wet Christmas."

She panted, "Right there." She tried to glide her tongue into my mouth, but I jerked back, not allowing her the satisfaction.

At least, not yet.

She whimpered in disapproval, craving my mouth.

My tongue.

My taste against hers.

Her pussy betrayed her, tightening around my fingers.

"Where, baby? Here?" Her wetness slipped down the palm of my hand, coating the sleeve of my Santa suit.

Body quivering…

Thighs trembling…

Hips starting to fuck my hand…

"Yes…"

So close to coming apart.

"Tell me, do you want me to put you over my knee?"

"No…"

"Then tell me, how many guys have you been with?"

NOELLE

I immediately opened my eyes. "Don't ask questions you don't want the answer to," I coaxed, hoping it would work.

"Is that right?" he asked in a devilish tone.

His eyes held nothing but mischief as his finger went right to my clit. He breathed into the side of my neck, making shivers crawl up my skin and throughout my entire body.

"You're not being a good girl..." He slapped my pussy, catching me off guard before returning right to work, and that was exactly what he was doing.

Working me over.

"That feel good, baby?" he rasped as he continued his assault on my clit.

"Yes..."

"Then answer the question, or I'll stop," he taunted.

"You wouldn't."

"Try me."

I recognized that tone, and I reluctantly gave in. "Three."

His eyes glazed over with a predatory expression that made me clench my thighs for a whole other reason.

He leaned forward, close to my mouth. "Did they make you come?"

"No."

His hand went back to my clit, manipulating me until my legs spread wider and wider for him. I was so close to release, rotating my hips against his hand. I wasn't lying. I dated three guys after him, and not one of them brought me close to orgasm. I mean, it felt good, but I couldn't get there without toys.

His mouth crashed onto mine, and we passionately kissed before I whimpered when he stopped. He kissed me one last time and moved his lips exactly where I wanted him.

Licking.

Sucking.

Tasting me in ways that had my eyes rolling to the back of my head.

I made all sorts of sounds I'd never heard before.

• • •

And I loved every second of it.

CHAPTER 16

NICHOLAS

I growled, instantly getting down on my knees and sucking her swollen clit into my mouth. I made her come on my face, squirting down my red beard. I bathed in her salty, musky sweetness, rubbing my face all over her pussy.

Lapping at her.

Drenching my lips.

Never taking my persistent tongue away from her clit, making her come with no end in sight.

"I can't... no more... please..." She begged for mercy.

"One more, give me one more."

And damn, she did.

Her juices dripped down the sides of my face, my throat, and onto my chest, soaking the front of my Santa suit.

Coming over and over again.

"Nicholas, please!"

"Fuck... Santa needs to feel you come down his sack."

I made her come so hard, her juices were dripping down my

beard. Her legs squeezed my face so damn hard that I had to lock my arms around her thighs to hold her down.

She finally came to when I was lying above her body, framing her in with my arms around her face.

Overpowering her.

Consuming her.

Claiming her the only way I knew how.

Her breathing was heavy and deep, her skin was bright pink, and she was slightly sweating. Her cinnamon scent was all around me, and she shined brightly with the afterglow of her orgasm. I would never tire of watching her come undone.

She was breathtaking.

"Well, Grinchy... your heart isn't the only thing growing three sizes this Christmas."

"Believe me, if you ever saw it, you would even say it glows."

She burst out laughing.

This was one of my favorite things about our relationship. We could go from such an intense moment to laughing with each other like it was nothing. It was easy.

"Nice wrapping, but I need to inspect it."

"So you do wanna Scrooge?"

She laughed again.

"I mean, you did wear the Santa suit. I guess it's the least I can do."

"And then what happens tomorrow?"

"You can buy me breakfast."

I smiled. "Then we're making it a not-so-silent night?"

"You don't even have to wrap your package for me."

I really smiled that time. "I've never—"

"Me neither, and I'm on the pill."

I didn't have to be told twice...

NOELLE

He mischievously grinned, crawling up my body, kissing and sucking his way up to my lips.

He kissed me hard.

Stifling my words.

My thoughts.

My entire being.

My tongue sought his out, and our kiss quickly turned into its own thing, like we were starving for one another.

Something was agonizing about the way we were moving. He caressed the side of my face, my breasts, and the back of my thighs like he didn't know where he wanted to touch me the most.

I placed my hand on his rapidly beating heart that was pounding against my chest, staring profusely into his eyes.

The devotion.

The adoration.

The love…

It was all there, staring right back at me.

"There she is … there's my girl."

He stripped out of his clothes, and I think I gasped a little when I saw the size of his North Pole. Emotions I'd never felt flew through me while he slowly crawled his way up my body again.

Taking what he wanted—no, needed—from me.

I was still wet, and in one rough thrust, he was deep inside me for the first time ever. His hips thrust harder and deeper into me with deliberate motion, knowing it felt amazing. I couldn't do anything but surrender to him.

Submit to the only man I ever loved.

My ex-best friend.

He adoringly kissed all over my face, along my jawline, my forehead, and on the tip of my nose. The room started spinning like it did when his face was between my legs. My head fell back, and my breathing became heady, urgent, and I felt so damn good…

He immediately lapped at my neck and breasts, leaving tiny marks all over. I didn't want to move. I wanted to enjoy the sensation of him being on top of me.

"That feel good, Elle?" He made his way back up to my mouth.

I nodded, unable to form words. My arms reached around him, hugging him closer against my body, wanting to feel all his weight on me. He leaned his forehead on mine and breathed out, "Open your eyes, look at me."

I did, taking in how lively, thriving, and full of love his stare reflected back into mine. Our mouths were parted, still touching and panting profusely.

"Fuck, yes, Noelle … just like that… Come on my cock… Give me what I want."

I was coming from my head down to my toes. Grabbing my leg, he inched it higher up his body.

"You like that?"

"Yes… Don't stop… Oh God."

"Jesus, you're so tight, so wet, so mine."

My entire world spun out of control, and so did his as I shuddered beneath him.

One thing was for sure.

I still loved him, but I couldn't say it yet.

Instead, I whimpered, "Swear?"

NICHOLAS

"All I want for Christmas is you."

The sensations of Noelle and only Noelle.

My mind reeled with so many emotions I couldn't keep up.

The feel of her.

The taste of her.

The smell of her.

Just her.

Always her.

Her pussy fit me like a glove, and I could have come right then and there. She moved her legs so that they were both wrapped around my lower back. Bringing me closer to her and hugging around my neck.

We kissed the entire time, not being able to get enough of each other. It seemed like hours went by, and the whole world was left behind us.

Where there was no history and all that was left was us.

"How do you do this to me? How have you always been able to do this to me?" she panted, her pussy pulsating down my shaft, tighter, making it hard to move.

"I'm going to come. Nicholas, please..."

"Please what?"

"Come with me." Her pussy clamped down, and I thrust in and out a few more times because she felt too good.

Until I couldn't hold back any longer and released my seed deep inside her.

Exactly where it belonged.

CHAPTER 17

NOELLE: THEN

It was junior year, and I made my way toward the concession stand at the rink, scanning the crowd, thinking maybe I'd found Nicholas among the people. The hockey game was over, and we won, thanks to my best friend.

For the next thirty minutes, I waited for him, but he was nowhere to be found.

Did he leave without me?

Before I could give it too much thought, I saw Nicholas from the corner of my eye. He stood by the cheerleaders, who paraded around him like always. Feeling tired, I decided to leave, and it wasn't until I gazed up that I realized I was suddenly lost.

Through my daze, I must have taken a wrong turn in the woods somewhere. Grabbing my cell phone from my back pocket, I went to call my dad, but it was dead. Instantly, I began retracing my steps. The dim lighting didn't help my disposition of trying to find my way back to the ice rink or home.

A snowmobile made its way in my direction.

They pulled up beside me, lifting their helmet in the air.

Nicholas smiled, nodding. "Come on."

It started snowing on our heads.

Handing me the other helmet, he added, "Let's go!"

I put on my helmet and hopped on the back of his mobile. He didn't waver, hitting the accelerator at full throttle, tearing through the snow. It was hard to see a foot in front of us.

By the time I coaxed, "Nicholas…"

We were already skidding across the road.

NICHOLAS

I was able to react and grab her before we crashed into the snow. The momentum of my snowmobile while it spun out of control helped tug her into my chest.

BANG!

The side of my bike slammed into a huge pile of snow, throwing us onto it. Thankfully, my body was able to break her fall, and she landed right on my chest.

"Oomph!" I wailed as the wind was knocked out of me immediately.

"Nicholas!" she shouted, slowly sitting up off my torso. "Oh my God!"

I couldn't find the words to speak, sucking in air that wasn't available for the taking. After what felt like an eternity, I began breathing normally.

"Are you okay?"

"I'm fine," I rasped, trying to sit up.

"You're not fine. You took a hard fall. Nicholas, you saved me. I landed right on you."

"Noelle," I sternly stated. "Just help me."

"Fine," she agreed.

Once I was upright, I called an Uber, and from the second she helped me onto her couch after he dropped us off at her house, I closed my eyes, breathing a sigh of relief. I was not sure how long I lay there when Noelle was suddenly handing me pain relievers in one hand and an ice pack in the other.

Thankfully, her dad was out of town.

Slowly, I sat up, groaning out in pain.

"Here."

I took them.

"Are you really okay?"

"Mm-hmm."

"Even if you weren't okay, you wouldn't tell me the truth, would you?"

"I don't lie to you."

"I find that hard to believe, but I'll accept it for now."

The look on her face was full of concern.

Confusion.

Longing.

Which made me question my resolve about how much I'd share with her at that moment.

Noelle

I changed into a hoodie and sweats. The uncomfortable silence hammered all around me, tearing into my insecurities about what was concerning him. Nicholas's body was in the room with me, but his mind was somewhere else entirely.

He looked lost.

I'd never seen that look on his face before.

The quietness was deafening, stirring me to ask, "What's wrong?" His eyes locked with mine as I sat in front of him on my bed.

He shrugged.

"Never mind, we don't have to tal—"

"I got in a fight with my parents before the game."

"Can I ask what happened?"

He thought about it for a second. I didn't think he'd reply.

"You know them, same ole, same ole. I'm just tired of not being good enough. They're always trying to change me into someone I'm not. It doesn't matter how many times I tell them I want to open my own construction business after we graduate, they don't care."

Chalk it up to hormones, or maybe it was me desperately wanting to connect with him. In that second, sitting in front of him, it felt like I was the first person he'd shared this with.

It seemed like he needed to get out whatever was weighing on him. His body shifted around as he abruptly looked deep into my eyes and searched for something I couldn't place. The only thing I could see was a war raging in his stare. An internal battle was taking place of what was right and what was wrong.

The serious expression on his face captivated me which only added to the plaguing emotions that were wreaking havoc between us. I waited on pins and needles, hanging on his every word.

He didn't make me wait too long, divulging, "I just want to be good enough for them."

I didn't move.

I was barely breathing.

Not wanting to distract him from sharing this with me.

"I can understand that."

I stood.

He looked at me with curiosity. "What are you doing?"

"Come on." Reaching for his arm, I placed it over my shoulders.

"Where are we going?"

"Just trust me, okay? I know what I'm doing."

Slowly, we walked out to porch under the snow.

We stayed there under the snow, letting it wash away the sadness.

I kissed his hand. "I don't like seeing you sad."

He didn't say a word. The stillness was nice. I felt him kiss the top of my head, and I smiled, aware that he was thanking me.

We stayed out there until it got to chilly, laughing it off.

However, our feelings for each other were now…

More than just under the mistletoe.

CHAPTER 18

NOELLE: NOW

W hen I was alone.
    With company.
Or with his brother.

Especially in moments like these when we were about to walk in the following night's festivities at his parents' estate.

Did I forget to mention my ex-best friend basically grew up in Santa's mansion?

The Saint Clair property was at the highest peak of the mountain in its own zip code. When I tell you his house was the size of a Walmart, I wasn't exaggerating in the least. I had so many memories with Nicholas on that property, especially during the holidays. The decorations his family put up every year were the talk of the town. They spent a small fortune on lights, globes, and lawn ornaments.

One year, they even had an anatomical Santa on their roof with all his reindeer, including Rudolph. It was custom-made to move in the most life-like way. Now, don't get me started on the Christmas trees all throughout the manor. Each one of them was themed in their own unique way. I spent so many nights hanging out with Nicholas, taking in the beauty of the holiday spirit around us.

However, that day, Nicholas spent most of it in meetings while I handled all the finishing touches on my dessert display for his parents' party. The whole town was invited; it was an open-door policy, and it had been so since before Nicholas was born. The Saint Clairs were huge on traditions.

Tomorrow was Christmas Eve, which was why his family threw their party on the same day every year. With a handful of gifts in tow, we made our way into his family's home. The guests participated in a purple elephant with a fifty-dollar minimum. Every year, Nicholas surprised me with the best presents, things I'd seen throughout the year that I wanted, and he'd pay attention to them without me even realizing he was doing so.

One year, it was this snow globe of The Rockefeller Center; another, it was a historical novel written by my favorite author, which was signed and personalized to me.

The best was when he reserved an air balloon ride over the town at dawn, and he actually went with me. To see the world come alive with him standing by my side was a memory I'd take to my grave. If I closed my eyes, I could still see us there on top of the world.

The man knew no bounds, and each year he proved how much he truly knew me.

His brother was the complete opposite of him, where Nicholas was sentimental; his brother was over the top. That was how different the brothers were.

I couldn't tell you how many times I contemplated calling him.

Writing.

Showing up at his home unannounced.

I never did.

I couldn't.

Rejection was a bitch, and I wasn't ready to have him tell me to go home or worse not answer me at all. Especially after his brother said he changed his phone number. I barely survived losing him the first time. There was no escaping my thoughts about him. Not when it came to him. The mere fact I was still thinking about him after all the years proved how much I still cared about him.

The more I tried to forget about him, the harder it was. Though in my heart, my soul, something was off. Almost overnight, his brother was kind of there for me in ways I didn't expect him to be. Almost like by Nicholas leaving, he made it easier for Felix to fill that void.

However, he couldn't hear Nicholas's name without tensing, spewing hate, or arguing with whoever brought him up.

I think, in a way, Nicholas became his rival in his own mind. I think it was because Nicholas was always the favorite, and everyone knew it too.

The longer we were together, the more apparent it became that maybe I was definitely in love with him.

I tried.

I begged.

I prayed.

When I looked into his eyes, all I saw was pain where there had once been so much affection.

Devotion.

Love.

Something had changed.

Even in the past couple of days, something was happening to him, and he couldn't fool me. He was enjoying this as much as he claimed that he wasn't.

My wants.

Needs.

Expectations.

This future I thought we'd never share felt as if it was at

arm's length now. Every time I thought he was maybe getting closer to his family, they were almost there, an issue would arise, and they'd find themselves on opposite sides of the fence, still looking toward a future they may never have.

Further and further, it flew out of their paths.

As much as I told myself not to do it, we texted all day. Flirting back and forth until I finally agreed to go to his parents' party with him. My crew was handling the event, so I could enjoy it. I had the best team, and I was beyond fortunate to have them on my side.

I couldn't stop thinking about three magic words all day.

I love you.

So many meanings.

So many ways to say it.

So many what-ifs and I-don't-knows.

I smiled every time a new text came through from him. He babysat the puppy for me most of the day, and I appreciated it. I still needed to come up with a name for him, but it was becoming obvious that not only was I getting attached to both of my rescued boys.

The Saint Clair family never did anything half-assed; this event was another outlandish celebration where they proved who was in power and needed to be respected among the community.

"Have I told you how beautiful you look tonight, Elle?" Nicholas wrapped his arms around my body from behind, tearing me away from my thoughts.

We were on the dance floor; suddenly, it felt as though all eyes were on us and the room. I spun around to face him, setting my hands on his solid chest. He was wearing a black suit, looking as handsome as ever. Reminding me why all the woman in the room couldn't take their eyes off him.

His greedy glare raked over the long red silk dress I was wearing. A romantic bow settled on the swell of my back, which was completely open. A live band performed while everyone danced around the big Christmas tree. "I'm Dreaming of a White Christmas" played from the speakers, setting up a dreamy aesthetic.

My dress curved perfectly around my body; it subtly flowed out down by my knees, and my hair was curled and tied to the right side of my head, with a few strands of hair framing my face. My makeup was heavy on the eyes, with black eyeliner and thick mascara. Some blush and a soft shade of nude for my pouty lips.

In a matter of a few seconds, his stare went from endearing like he was trying to make a memory of me to predatory.

"My brother won't stop staring at you."

I asked, "Are you trying to pick a fight with him? You still haven't told me what last night was about."

"It doesn't matter. I have the girl."

I smiled.

"But I'd love for you to tell me what happened between you two."

I shook my head, understanding the sharp tone in his voice. "It's not like that between Felix and me."

"He seems to think so."

Nicholas grabbed my hand, molding me close to his body, pulling me tighter into his strong, muscular frame. He guided my arms up around his neck with no space between us before wrapping his arms around me, proving my point.

"Just dance with me."

I swallowed hard and nodded at his request, not wanting to make a scene when everyone was happy and enjoying themselves at the party. Sighing in defeat, I laid my cheek on his chest, and he placed his chin on top of my head.

"All I've ever wanted was you."

I repeated, needing to know. "What did you say to him?"

"The truth."

"Which is what? What's the truth?"

He smiled wide. "That you rode my face."

I sighed. "I figured that's what you told him."

"And you're disappointed?"

"No."

He leaned, breathing into my ear. "Look, I'm sorry, all right?" His easy smile was back, his eyes drilling into mine like he needed me to believe him. "He'd been drinking—"

"You know what they say; a drunk person speaks the truth."

"Then you should start drinking so I can get it from you."

The conflicting emotions came tumbling down on me, crippling me. I suddenly needed some fresh air and a moment to myself.

To think.

To breathe.

I hated showing weakness in front of anyone. Before he could throw more questions at me, I snapped around, making my way toward the outside rose garden.

Inhaling a long, deep, sturdy breath, I stood in front of the fountain in the center of the garden, trying to distract myself with the water and the soft glow it gave everything around me. Usually, this view would have me awestruck and at peace, but I couldn't stop the emotions consuming my mind and body.

And then just like that, it unexpectedly changed…

Out of nowhere, his grandmother stood beside me.

CHAPTER 19

NOELLE

I hadn't seen her since her husband's funeral. She was the sweetest woman and had been since the moment I met her. Where his parents and grandfather were firm and hard on Nicholas, his grandmother was the angel among the chaos.

"You look beautiful, but you always do," she greeted with a loving expression.

"Thank you. You look amazing too."

She smiled, sitting down on the edge of the fountain.

"Nicholas's grandfather bought this dress for me years ago. I haven't worn it since, and I thought tonight would be a good occasion to wear it in his memory. He said it brought out my eyes."

"It does."

"You and Nicholas seem awfully chummy." She set her hands on her lap. "But then again, my grandson has always been smitten with you, and I know you know that."

I shook my head. "I'm not sure how long I've known that, though."

"Love is complicated sometimes."

"It can be."

"Nicholas looks good," she remarked as if I had something to do with that. "He's happy to be home. This is where he belongs."

"I wish he knew that."

She nodded. "He does."

"I don't know about that."

"He's just stubborn like his grandfather... I knew when I told him that Nicholas will inherit—"

"Wait, you're the one who wanted him to own Mistletoe Town?" I questioned, interrupting her.

"Of course."

I wasn't expecting her to say that.

"Wow."

"Why is that so surprising, dear?"

I shrugged. "You've just always been so supportive of Nicholas, and I didn't think you'd want him to own something that he clearly never wanted."

The concerned expression on her face quickly shifted to endearment. Her eyes always lit up when she talked about her grandson. She lit up when she talked about all her family, but with Nicholas it was different. He was special to her.

"Nicholas has yet to figure out he can do both."

"What do you mean both?"

"He can relocate his company here."

"I thought his grandfather didn't want him to do that."

She smirked. "His grandfather is no longer here, and it wasn't that he didn't want him to open his own business. It was more like he wanted him to follow in his footsteps. Forgive me for saying this, but my husband was a hard-ass when it came to not getting his way. That was why he was such a successful businessman. He never took no for an answer, and I believe Nicholas was the first to ever do so."

"Does he know that?"

"Yes, but I know in my heart he'll come around to the idea of him owning a piece of paradise and also his business that he's worked so hard for. Especially after you guys get married and have kids. Who knows…" She winked at me. "You might be pregnant already."

I gasped. "Oh…"

She smirked again. "So, you have been sleeping with my grandson?"

"I… I… I…"

"It's okay, darling. I may be old, but I'm not old enough not to realize you two are in love, and I couldn't approve more."

My gaze widened. "Really?"

"Absolutely. You were made for each other. You always have been. All I've ever wanted is for my family to be happy, and now that the love of my life is gone, I'm making sure that my family will be okay once I'm gone too. It's on my shoulders to make that happen."

"I understand wanting to feel that way."

She reached for my hands as if we were just two schoolgirls gossiping.

With the warmest smile, she announced, "You're the key that holds Nicholas's heart and the key to his Christmas. You're his home, Noelle. You've always been his home. Wherever you are, he'll be happy. Because at the end of the day, you hold his Grinch heart."

Before I could reply, she pulled me into a tight hug. Like a mother-type hug. I leaned into her embrace, feeling the love she was pouring.

"I didn't know I needed to hear this until right now. Thank you, Mrs. Saint Clair."

She kissed my cheek and left.

Once she was gone, *he* approached me from behind, and I didn't have to turn around to know who it was. I heard his footsteps follow, bringing him closer to where I stood before the fountain. My breathing hitched as soon as I felt him come up behind my shaky frame. I didn't turn around; I didn't move. I closed my eyes but didn't know what I was waiting for. His warmth increased the closer he got, convincing me I would combust at any moment.

We weren't even touching, yet his presence engulfed me.

Owned me.

He was everywhere.

His hands.

His lips.

His love.

He leaned in just inches away, letting his whiskey breath brush against my ear and assault all my senses. Shivers coursed through me and down my spine while my knees buckled.

I wrapped my arms around my stomach, trying to hold in the emotions that threatened to spill, knowing he noticed. There was no way he couldn't have felt the effect he always had over me.

His touch.

His aura.

His mere presence.

My breath hitched as I shuddered, and weakened, the wall I built came tumbling down at our feet.

"I have a gift for you," he stated out of nowhere.

"Nicholas—"

"It's tradition. You get a gift tonight, on Christmas Eve, and on Christmas morning."

I swallowed hard, not knowing what to say or do. I should have left, but I couldn't get my feet to move. They were glued to the ground, cemented into this place and time where it felt so good to have him there with me after all this time.

I licked my lips, my mouth suddenly becoming dry.

My head spun in a whirlwind of feelings, battling with my

heart to move or to stay grounded. I wanted to turn and face the man who was still such a mystery to me although before I could, his actions decided for me.

My eyes followed the quick movement of his strong arms as they came around my body. Skimming the sides of my ribs, he placed his hands on the railing out in front of me, which protected the fountain from intruders.

He caged me in against his body, his scent, his suit.

Engulfing me.

Comforting me.

Tormenting.

It was loud.

Explosive.

Maddening.

It was everything.

CHAPTER 20

NICHOLAS

The closer he got to me, the more I wanted to feel him against my body. I yearned to be touched in a way I knew he could soothe me. I sensed he wanted to put his hands on me, and I needed to feel my silky skin under his callused fingers.

He didn't.

"Open it," he whispered, indicating his gift, a slender box wrapped in paper, covered in silver foil, and tied with a pretty white bow.

I did, allowing my fingers to linger with his for a couple of seconds. Opening the jewelry box, I gasped as soon as I saw the rose gold locket necklace. I had my eyes on it for the past year.

How did he know?

"How did you know?" I asked. "How do you always know what to get me?" I had to finally know the answer to a question plaguing my mind for as long as I could remember.

"Because I know you," he emphasized, placing his hands over mine, and I jumped from his sudden touch.

I could feel him grinning, knowing he was the cause of the

rapid rhythm beating against the palm of his hand. Slowly, he opened the locket with my hands in his, and that warm feeling washed over me. It had the perfect photo of my mom that immediately melted my heart. It was my favorite picture of her.

I had no words.

He rendered me speechless.

All I had were emotions spilling out.

His hand rose to the side of my cheek.

I was feeling so much…

Yet not nearly enough.

I sucked in a breath when he took the locket out of my hands and placed it around my neck.

"There. Now it's where it's meant to be."

It was then that I couldn't take it any longer.

It was then that it became too much.

It was then that I may have ruined the moment…

NICHOLAS

Her lower lip trembled. "What happens now? You leave, and I don't see you again for how long? Are you here to say goodbye? How does the rest of this play out?"

There was so much emotion behind her gaze. I knew they mirrored mine. Our eyes spoke for themselves as I took her face between my hands and caressed the sides of her cheeks with my thumbs.

My thoughts.

My words.

They all seemed to be intertwined with one another, pushing and pulling like a game of tug of war.

"What do you want from me?" she whispered, peering into my chest.

I lifted her chin so I could once again look into her beautiful eyes. The pain in her voice was tangible like I could reach out and touch it, obliterate it with my bare hands and replace it with something else—anything else.

"Whatever you have to give me," I answered simply, wiping away the tears from her cheeks.

Her lips started quivering, unable to form words. I kissed her forehead, resisting the urge to claim every last inch of skin.

One of my biggest regrets in my life was leaving her...

"I can't lose you again," I stated the truth.

"You don't have me now."

"I forgot how adorable you are when you lie." I nodded, looking deep into her eyes. "You're in my arms, so I'll take you any way I can."

A frown pinched her face as she pulled away from me, shaking her head. Breaking our connection.

Both our stares darted in the direction it came from.

"Am I interrupting?"

Still, I couldn't get my gaze to move.

Refocus.

Connect to my brother.

With wide eyes, I stepped back, replying, "We were just leaving."

He spoke up. "You should go inside and say hello to the family."

I nodded.

He was right.

But at least this time...

I had her by my side.

A few men in suits were scattered around as we made our way back inside, drinking, watching while scantily-clad women danced around. The only upside for my brother was that he knew I didn't want to own the power. I was better at getting my hands dirty than I was running behind the scenes.

I nodded at Alfred. "He in there?"

He grinned. "When is he not in?"

The library was massive, with a black leather couch to the right. Floor-to-ceiling bookcases surrounded the room, and a wet bar stood near the mahogany desk. Everyone stood around, shooting the shit.

I narrowed my eyes, examining my father's perfect posture while tilting my head.

"Getting started without me?" I asked, trying to break the ice.

I lifted my glass.

He lifted his. "What can I say? It's the holidays."

I braced myself for what would come next.

Ready.

Willing.

Eager to get this over with.

To my surprise, my father stated, "I've been hearing good things, and I saw the pictures of you last night. You looked like you were enjoying yourself."

"Debatable," I joked.

"I'm going to use the bathroom," Noelle informed. "I'll be back."

Looking over his shoulder and back at me, Dad added, "She's a woman you can't control, no matter how hard you try. She pulls you in and makes you both weak and strong. It could go both ways, Nicholas. You either get the girl with the town or you—"

"Or I what?"

"For what it's worth." He tilted his head. "She's good for you."

"I don't know what you're talking about."

He threw his head back and laughed. "The only time your lies are shit are when they're about her. And I said what I said. She's good for you. She always has been."

"That's the first you've ever mentioned it before."

"Better late than never."

I narrowed my eyes at him.

"It's good to see you home, Nicholas."

I jerked back.

"Don't look so surprised. Of course I'm thrilled my son is home."

"You're not upset over what grandfather—"

"No. I'm not."

"I find that hard to believe."

"Why is that?"

"You do remember the last time we were in this room?"

"Yes…" I never expected what he exclaimed next, "And I've lived with the regret of it ever since."

CHAPTER 21

NICHOLAS: THEN

"Nicholas," Dad warned. "How many times have I told you you're going to start working for Mistletoe Town?"

"More than I care to remember," I snapped.

The biggest problem with my old man and me was we were so different yet exactly alike.

His stubbornness.

His controlling ways.

His trait of always having to be right no matter what.

Though when he loved, he loved with everything inside him.

Yeah, I checked all those boxes too.

"Why must you fight me on everything?" he argued, tugging me away from my thoughts. "Why is it so hard for you to listen to me?"

He shook his head with disappointment spreading all over his face like a blazing wildfire. An expression you'd think I'd be used to by now.

Nothing I did was ever good enough. His high expectations

made it nearly impossible to please him. Everything, and I mean everything, in life was black and white for him.

I was the only gray area in his world of right or wrong.

"How many times do I have to tell you I want to open my own business after I graduate in a month?"

"It's not going to happen."

"Why are you so against me having my own life?"

"Because I'm handing you one where you'll immediately be successful! Why would you want to work from the ground up if you don't have to? This is your legacy! Why can't you just see that? You refuse to let me help you!"

"That isn't saving me! That's you not believing in me and what I'm capable of without your help!"

"Son," Grandma intervened, saving my ass.

She did this often, having to come between her son and grandson.

Two of the men she loved more than anything constantly butted heads. It never mattered how much trouble I got in. She always loved me wholeheartedly. She was patient with me. Something my father clearly didn't have when it came to me.

I didn't wanna continue arguing with my father, not with my grandmother there. More often than not, she took my side, reminding him I was born with my own personality and didn't have to be obsessed with Christmas.

My mind was wired differently.

"You need to calm down."

"Mom," Dad stressed in a sharp tone. "Calm down? Calm down?! He knows where his place is, and that's in Mistletoe Town! Why would you want to struggle?"

My stomach somersaulted. My emotions were running so high. I couldn't keep having the same fight with him over and over again. Not only was it not healthy, but I was beyond over it.

"This is the only way I know how to be!"

"Look at you! Just look at you, Nicholas! You're a Saint Clair!

Don't you understand that? You think I'm trying to punish you, but don't for one second think I didn't do that for you! I will not stand by while you ruin your life! I'm your father! You're my son! My job is to protect you! No matter what!"

"Protect me? From what exactly, huh? Living my own life? My own dreams?"

"Nicholas, please..." Grandma pleaded, standing in front of me with tears in her eyes. "Don't do this. I'm begging you, please don't do this."

"Do what? Tell the truth?"

He growled, loud and clear.

"All you've ever done is kill my dreams! You don't want a son; you want a puppet!"

He scoffed out a breath, shaking his head.

"He loves you. You're the most important thing to him in the world."

"He has a horrible way of showing it."

"He's just trying to do what's best for you. It's a tough place for any parent to be in."

"No," I sternly replied. "I just wanna live my life. I don't care about the consequences."

"All I've ever done," my father insisted, "is try to help you make the right decisions. Be someone who shows you the way, but it was never good enough. It's never been good enough for you. You've resisted me at every turn, at every step! You have no idea the things I've done to support and help you because you refuse to see them."

"You know what?"

"What?"

"I don't have to deal with this anymore. If you refuse to let me open my own building business in Mistletoe Town, then I'll just leave."

"Nicholas!" Grandma scolded. "Take that back! You don't mean that! Tell him you don't mean that!"

"I've always known he's wanted me to be someone I'm not. He wanted me to be born different since day one. The truth is he hates who I am, and we both know it!"

"That's not true. Your father loves you. He loves you more than anything in this world."

"Yeah? Well, like I said—he has a horrible way of showing it."

"I expressed it to you the only way I knew how!"

"It's not your choice to make. I've worked to give you everything you've wanted. Be the perfect son, but I won't give in to this!"

"You couldn't be more wrong. I may not have been the father you think I should have been or should be, but I know when you took your first step, when you lost your first tooth, and when you got your first haircut! I know about every skinned knee, every bruise, every broken bone, every runny nose, every milestone in your life. Why? Because I was there.

"That's not what's important right now! You totally missed the point. Why am I not surprised? None of that matters to me, but the one thing that does, you couldn't care about. You have the bar set so high for what you think I should be, there's no way I could ever reach it. It's not the same for Felix or Holly like it is for me."

"Couldn't be further from the truth."

"I don't know what hurts worse—you not supporting me or that you don't believe in me."

"I just want what's best for you. It's all I've ever wanted."

I held my head higher.

"Your grandfather is right, Nicholas."

My eyes narrowed, drifting my stare toward her.

"I'm sorry, but I can't do this anymore." I stood taller. "After I graduate next…"

In four words, I changed the course of my life. "I'm leaving Mistletoe Town."

"If you do… don't bother coming back! Do you understand me? We're done. You want your own life, then consider yourself a loner."

My mouth dropped before I scoffed. "I can't believe you."

"Believe it."

"Nicholas, he doesn't mean—"

I kissed my grandmother on the cheek and got the hell out of there. My immediate thought was Noelle and how there was no doubt in my mind that she would leave with me.

Right?

I decided not to tell her right then what was going on like I usually did. Instead, I needed to devise a plan or at least some sort of dialogue of how I'd bring this up to her. It had to be the perfect timing.

Today wasn't that day, but soon…

I'd ask her to leave with me.

Never expecting her to say no.

CHAPTER 22

NICHOLAS: NOW

"That was a long time ago," Dad chimed in.

I nodded. "Yeah, it was."

"A lot has changed since then."

"I agree."

"You know when your grandfather told me that he was going to leave you Mistletoe Town, I thought to myself almost immediately how everything happens for a reason."

"I had no idea this was going to happen. You think maybe someone could have given me a warning?"

"Like who? Noelle? Should we have used her to bring you back sooner? Because from the looks of it, she seems to be working her magic on you."

"That noticeable, huh?"

"Son, I saw you dressed as Santa Claus. It doesn't get more real than that."

I chuckled. It was crazy to have this normal conversation with my father, considering how we left things between us.

"What can I say? Your baker has the power of persuasion."

"She sure seems to have that effect on my sons, but Felix never stood a chance, and I think he's realizing that."

"She's... I don't even know how to explain it other than she's literally this Christmas light shining bright in my face, making me feel all warm and well... this sense of holiday spirit seems to be working its way through me whether I want it to or not."

"You've always liked Christmas, Nicholas. I've seen your face when you were a kid. You just fought it to fight me."

"Dad, I—"

"No, Nicholas," Grandma intervened, suddenly standing beside us.

We seemed to clear the room, and only we were left there with our past playing out before us.

"You need to let your father finish what he has to say," she ordered, bringing my attention back to him.

"What is she talking about?"

"I was just about to go looking for you, but I found Felix first."

"Is that why he told me to come say hello to you?"

"Yes," Felix added, walking into the room with his hands in the pockets of his slacks. "When grandfather first told me you'd be taking over this town, I thought to myself, damn... even in death he was going to give you what is most sacred to him."

"Felix, you know I don't—"

"That's what makes it worse, and now you have my girl too."

I shook my head. "She was never your girl."

"If you break her heart again, I'll break your face."

At that moment, I started seeing my brother as a loved one versus someone I didn't get along with.

"Noted," I replied, nodding.

"Anyway," he added. "As I was saying, the news hit me like a ton of bricks, and I've tried not to hate you ever since."

"When did you—"

"A few years ago, I was grabbing something off his desk and his will was on the computer screen. I couldn't help myself. There in front of my eyes was your name."

My eyes widened.

"I never told grandfather I knew until he told us a few months ago."

"I see…"

"Do you? Because from where I'm standing, you're one lucky son of a bitch."

I nodded because he was right, and I couldn't argue with that.

"And not only do you have Mistletoe Town but you also have a thriving construction business."

"I've worked my ass off for that."

"So I've heard."

"Care to elaborate?"

"I did some research," he shared. "I'm sure we all did."

From an outsider looking in, I did have everything I set my mind to except one thing…

"I do have a lot, but the most important thing I don't have is family. Do you understand how hard that's been for me?"

"Two wrongs don't make a right," Grandma insisted, and I couldn't argue with that either.

I still talked to my family. I even saw them a few times when they came to visit.

However, our relationship was strained.

At first, I changed my phone number. I mostly did that due to the fact that I didn't want them finding me to try to change my mind. Over the course of a few months, I finally snapped out of it and called them. It was touch and go there for a minute, but now we talked every so often.

It still wasn't good enough.

It never was.

Not holding back, I confessed, "I miss you guys. I hope you at least know that."

"Oh, Nicholas..." Grandma pulled me into a tight hug. "I'm so happy you're home."

My mother made her way into the large space, kissing me on the cheek with a nostalgic smile clear across her face.

"We've all missed you," she coaxed, pulling me into another tight hug.

I hugged her back. It felt good to be in her arms.

"Despite what happened, we're very proud of everything you've accomplished, and now that you're home, I'm hoping we can take the steps to move in the right direction."

"Yes," Grandma agreed with my mom. "Especially if you're going to have a baby!"

"What?" Mom smiled, beaming.

What the hell is going on?

I opened my mouth to argue, but I closed it instead.

The thought of Noelle pregnant with my baby made my heart race...

"Is she pregnant?" Mom followed up, way to overly excited. "Oh, I'd love a baby in this house! We're long overdue!"

"He just got here!" Felix exclaimed. "He can't work that fast."

Or can I?

Speaking of the devil, Noelle walked in with Holly beside her. My little sister wasn't so little anymore.

"Nicholas!" She rushed over to me, wrapping her arms tightly around my chest. "I'm so happy you're here! It's been way too long."

The emotions that poured out of me in that second weren't something I expected to happen this soon, but they were unintentionally laying it on thick.

"I missed you too." I kissed the top of her head.

Noelle stopped dead in her tracks, taking in the vision in

front of her before hiding a smile behind her hand. She couldn't fool me. It didn't matter how nonchalant she pretended to be, I knew how much she enjoyed this.

Fully aware everything was getting to me.

Including envisioning her pregnant with my baby.

It wasn't as if we were getting any younger, and she was my best friend. In a matter of seconds, my life with her flashed before my eyes.

Her.

Me.

A puppy.

Mistletoe Town.

A baby...

The thought of her carrying my kid stirred my dick, and I realized all too soon we needed to go.

"Let me take a picture of you guys," Noelle ordered, directing everyone to the main Christmas tree.

She set us beside each other by age order, meaning I had to wrap my arm around my brother. To my surprise, he did it first. My sister leaned into me, and we all smiled like one big happy family.

Although there was a long road ahead of us.

The future looked merry and bright.

CHAPTER 23

NOELLE

I woke up in Nicholas's arms again, with the puppy sleeping in the nook of his arm.

"You're going to spoil him." I smiled, not caring in the least.

"Too late for that."

"He's supposed to be sleeping in his crate."

"He wasn't into that idea."

"Oh… so you're owned by a cockapoo now?"

"I guess so." He smiled. "He needs a name. What do you think about Maximillian?"

The puppy's head perked up as soon as he heard his name. "Well, looks like he has chosen."

He brought him up to kiss his face. There was something about a man and a puppy. I swear my heart was exploding.

"So, he's like Max 2.0?"

"He's in memory of Max. We have Maximillian."

"That we're still going to call Max?"

"Mm-hmm…"

I giggled. "I'll go with it, but only since Max approved."

He was relentless in his pursuit of trying to win me over, and I stopped fighting it. I was so happy.

Moving half of his body off me, I tried to get up, but he wrapped his arm around my stomach.

"Where do you think you're going?" he hazily questioned, pulling me back toward him and engulfing me with his addicting scent again. He tucked me into his chest.

Slowly, he ran his nose along the back of my neck. "I always love the feel of you in the morning," he groggily added, brushing his lips against my back.

"It's excruciating," I sassed, teasing him.

Before he could object, I propelled my body forward and rushed out of the bed, taking the bedsheet with me. Except that left him only in gym shorts in front of me.

My gaze greedily took him in.

From his chiseled chest.

To his rock-hard abs.

Down to the V above his dick.

Which was just as hard as his abs, standing straight at attention.

I licked my lips.

You'd think he'd have some sort of modesty, but nope. He didn't know the meaning of the word. He simply sat up against the headboard, placing his arms behind his head.

"Since you're staring right at my cock, why don't you just come ride it instead?"

"Merry Christmas Eve to you too…"

"Are you Christmas? Because I want to Merry you."

I laughed. "You're the reason Santa even has a naughty list. Now, you need to cover yourself. I have an appointment for a massage this morning that I can't get out of. They should be here any minute."

He arched an eyebrow.

"Relax, Mr. Saint Clair. Your office staff has gotten me a

massage every Christmas Eve morning for the past couple of years because they know what tomorrow brings."

"I never understood why everyone had to work on Christmas Day when they should be with their families."

"Because Christmas, Mr. Grinch, is about giving, not receiving, and that's what this town stands for."

"You've had no problem receiving all the orgasms I've so generously been giving you."

"See…" I baited. "Look how great you are at the giving, and you will be all about the giving tomorrow when you help me in my bakery."

"Oh, am I?"

"Oh, yes." I wiggled my eyebrows. "We have lots of cookies to bake."

"As long as there isn't a raisin in sight, we won't have a problem."

I grabbed Max out of his arms. "Your daddy does not like raisins."

Shit…

It just slipped out.

"I mean… I didn't—"

He stood, placing his fingers over my mouth. "I like it when you call me daddy."

My mouth dropped open.

Reaching for Max, he started backing him away when he added, lifting Max in the air. "This is a good place to start."

With that, he simply turned and left.

We stayed at his house, and I texted the therapist, telling them I was next door and to come there instead. After I undressed and wrapped a blanket around my body, I walked into the bathroom, closing the door behind me. I tried preparing for my massage by relaxing in the warm water, which felt amazing on my sore muscles for a few minutes.

Nicholas was definitely giving me one hell of a workout. My

body was sore in places I didn't even know one could be sore. Once I was dry, I rubbed some face cream, threw on a robe, and then made my way back into the living room.

I smiled when I saw the massage table ready for me near his Grinch tree. It was perfect. The lights were shining. I loved it. Last night went amazing with this family, and I couldn't have been happier for him. They all seemed ready to leave the past behind them and move to a healthier place where they could be a loving family again.

I knew how much they missed him. How much they regretted how everything went down between them. I hated that they spent all those years worrying about him and not being able to do much about it.

I tossed my robe on one of the couches, then settled onto the table with the blanket covering the lower half of my body.

"I'm ready!" I shouted, assuming they were in the bathroom, getting prepared.

Moments later, I heard footsteps coming toward me.

"My neck and shoulders are killing me, but so are my lower back and inner thighs," I informed. "I prefer a firm hand too. Don't be afraid to get in there deep. I can take it." I closed my eyes the second I felt their hands on my shoulders. "Oh, gosh…" I quietly moaned. "That feels perfect."

I was in my own little world, where all my senses were alert and aching around me. I could tell I had a male massage therapist based on how big his hands were. He eased his way down my back, and I couldn't help it. I groaned again.

I was one of those women who was a bit vocal when she received a massage. I wasn't expecting to feel that much intensity from him touching me, but his hands were wonderful, only leaving a trail of heat that awakened my body with his strong movements.

He worked my neck for a bit before moving toward my lower back. I didn't say anything when he slid the blanket down to the middle of my butt cheeks, thinking he was going to work that area. He did, kneading with his knuckles at first. It wasn't until he began sliding the blanket farther down my ass that I felt a little too comfortable with him.

I opened my eyes, seeing his feet.

I recognize those feet.

Since he wanted to pretend he was a massage therapist, I was going to give him one hell of a performance.

"Your hands feel amazing," I practically moaned. "I've never had hands like this before."

I lightly whimpered when he dug his knuckle into the knot on my neck. I smiled to myself. I was getting to him.

"Do you think you could work my inner thighs? I'm super sore there."

He did, getting close to my core.

"A little higher."

He did.

"A bit more."

He did, and now he was an inch away from my pussy.

"Yeah, but there… better yet, maybe you should rub between my legs… I'm pretty sore there too."

In the blink of an eye, the blanket was off my ass, and he spanked me hard.

"I'm kidding!" I immediately gave in. "I know it's you!"

"I know you know it's me." Another smack.

"Hey! You're the one who sent my massage therapist away. How rude."

"I paid for his time and even bought this table from him. He was more than fine."

"So then he was good-looking?"

One more smack.

Taking a deep breath, I shook my head. "You're unbe-lievable!"

Inching higher, he rubbed closer to my core. The touch of his hands continued their exploration of my limbs, and it ignited my nerve endings into nothing but desire.

"Then I'm doing my job."

"What's your job exactly?"

"Keeping my girl satisfied."

"I'm your girl now?"

"You've always been my girl."

As soon as the last word left his mouth, he flipped me over and began caressing my breasts in soft but demanding touches. The lotion he was using made it easier for him to slide up and down my breasts to the sides of my stomach.

I let out a heady moan, loving the way his hands felt on me. I'd never tire of this man. Not wasting any time, he caressed my nub, triggering me to suck in a breath. He stayed there for a minute before he readily slipped two fingers inside me while his other hand pushed against my lower stomach.

"What are you do—"

"Relax."

Gliding his fingers in and out of me, he didn't move his hand from my stomach, and he continued to push down as he fingered me. "Oh God..."

The pressure he was applying with his hand on my belly made the way he was fingering me that much more intense. It was only a matter of minutes before my body was convulsing, contracting, and shaking as he fingered me faster and harder.

It was an overload of sensations.

I could physically feel my core pushing his fingers out, but he didn't let up, fingering me deeper until my entire body came with such force I trembled uncontrollably.

"Good girl," he praised.

He straddled my waist and cupped my breasts, then slid his dick between them. Back and forth, he slid his cock between my breasts. I whimpered when he backed away, but my disappointment didn't last long. He bent forward and kissed my mouth while he stroked his cock.

I moved his hand and stroked him.

He groaned as I twirled my grasp around his shaft.

Never once did he stop devouring my mouth.

He thrust two fingers inside me, going straight for my G-spot that was still sensitive. The raw uninhibited craving to cum again hit me like a ton of bricks, and before my core contracted, he grabbed his dick and thrust inside me.

I felt full like my body was made for him.

"Oh God, please don't stop. Harder... ahh ... yes ... yes ... just like that."

"There's my girl."

I wanted it rough.

Hard.

Demanding.

I wanted him to brand me.

Mark me.

Make me his.

"Tell me you love my cock inside you. Tell me you never want me to stop fucking you. Tell me, or I'll stop and leave you like this."

The familiar response of wanting to cum made its way down my core, and I started to come apart again.

"Yes..." That was all I could muster, not wanting to use the word love with him.

Our breathing and panting were in sync. It only took a few more thrusts, grunts, and groans, and we came at the exact same time.

"You're mine, Noelle Woods. All mine." His tone was laced with pure possession.

And I allowed myself to get lost in him.

. . .

In us.

CHAPTER 24

NOELLE

I thought about how much my life had changed and what was yet to come. For some reason, it all hit me that morning. Christmas was tomorrow and I had no idea what happened next.

Was he really staying?

My hand slid up and down my stomach, contemplating what his grandmother said and the possibility of already being pregnant.

I chuckled to myself.

People in relationships talked about these things during the dating phase. Getting to know each other and what the other wanted for their future. We skipped that whole stage, jumping headfirst into having sex, but we already knew everything about each other.

We weren't strangers by any means.

A look.

A word.

A smile.

His scent.

His kiss.

His hands all over my body.

I couldn't keep up with the emotional highs and lows. There was no hiding from it, seeing it for what it was.

We were happy, laughing, in love...

I never imagined I'd be living a life that appeared to be someone else's.

The rumbling of a snowmobile pulled me away from my thoughts as I sat at the window, looking at the tree with Max in my arms. Nicholas ran out to grab something he said he left at the office. I sat up and gazed behind me as I heard the bike get closer to the house. Stepping into my boots next, I stood and walked toward the street.

"What is your dad up to?" I asked Max, realizing very quickly I used that word again.

In front of my eyes, the past and present collided with such force that I couldn't help but smile. Once Nicholas noticed I was standing there, he stopped the snowmobile and took off his helmet. With an intense stare, he left me speechless. His gaze spoke volumes without having to say a word as he sat there on the mobile.

Breaking our trancelike state, I questioned, "You went to pick up a snowmobile from your parents?"

"Nah," he expressed. "I bought this one for you. Merry Christmas Eve."

For the second time that day, my mouth dropped open.

He beamed, all proud of himself.

"Now you're spoiling me."

"Get used to it." He grinned. "I'm back, baby. Now let's go for a ride."

I narrowed my eyes at him. "I'm not going to pretend that seeing you on that snowmobile doesn't affect me. I practically lived on the back of yours."

There was a permanent grin on his face. "Why do you think I bought it for you?"

I laughed, hurrying back inside. I got Max nice and comfy in his crate. He loved it in there and I made sure the doggie cam was working.

"Be back soon, Maximillian!"

I hauled ass outside and grabbed the extra helmet from Nicholas's hands, then put it on while I jumped on the seat.

I ordered, "Take me for a ride, Mr. Saint Clair."

He didn't have to be told twice. For the next hour, we drove all over the woods. We were back to being those kids again. The ones who were wild and free. I loved every second of that afternoon with him.

It was perfect.

He was perfect.

Veering off on a secluded road, he drove us back to where I didn't think he'd go. Right when he parked the snowmobile, he turned me to straddle his waist.

Instantaneously, I remembered all the times we'd talk just like this.

"The more things change," I stated, "the more they stay the same."

I looked around the space. We were in our woods, the one where he made the gingerbread house for me for my year anniversary of living there with him.

Except that wasn't the only thing; it was completely decked out with all the decorations again.

"How did you do this?"

"I had help."

My eyebrows rose.

"My personal assistant made some calls and found someone for me. She's been working on it since my plane landed."

"Nicholas…"

"I knew I'd get you back here, and I had to make sure it'd be right. I'm sorry I didn't do it myself this time, but I will next year." He gripped the back of my neck. "And the next year and the following." Before he softly pecked my lips. "And the next…"

"That's a lot to commit to."

"Mm-hmm…"

Clutching onto the side of my face with his other hand, he lightly bit my bottom lip. His hands fell to my ass, gripping it nice and tight.

The memory of him never compared to real life.

I moaned into his mouth, and he groaned into mine.

He fisted my hair by the nook of my neck while his other hand glided down the side of my body.

"Please," I pleaded against his mouth, fully aware he'd love to hear me beg for it.

He roughly jerked my hair back to look into my lust-filled glare. When his fingers slid my panties over, I swallowed hard. With nothing but mischief in his green, tantalizing stare, he slid his hand into the snow overalls I was wearing.

I hissed upon contact. His hands were freezing.

"I'll warm you right up."

I leaned in to kiss him again, but he pulled my hair back harder, urging me to stay right where I was, spread wide open for him. It was only then I realized he wanted to watch me fall apart from his skilled, precise fingers.

I swear I could have cum from the powerful.

Greedy.

Loving the way he was looking at me.

He rubbed back and forth over my clit, causing my body to shudder from his firm, demanding touch.

When he slid two fingers inside me, I breathed out, "Ahhhh."

His lips parted like he was feeling everything I was, and all he was doing was watching me fall over the edge for him.

He worked me over, finding my G-spot.

Creating this ache.

This passion.

This mind-blowing explosion all over my pussy.

I tried to keep my fluttering eyes open while he roughly fingered me.

"That feel good, Elle?"

"Yes," I panted, completely at his mercy.

"Here?" he taunted, pushing harder against my sweet spot.

"Yes ... please don't stop..."

My back arched over the gas tank, allowing him to go faster and harder. He was right. I felt warm all over with the uncontrollable yearning to take away the throbbing ache he was building inside me.

"Oh God... go faster ... harder..."

"Tell me, have you ever had someone claim your ass?"

I sucked in a rapid breath. "No…"

He smiled against my mouth.

"Can you…?"

"Can I just what? What can I do for my girl?"

I moaned, "Make me cum, please..."

"One last question."

I whimpered.

"Have you ever had a man make love to you?"

I shook my head. "No."

"Good girl. Now cum for me."

My body erupted in a fit of spasms as my eyes rolled to the back of my head, and my breathing hitched, screaming out his name. He pulled me close, wrapping my arms around his neck to kiss me, and drowned out the loud sounds escaping my mouth.

Biting my bottom lip again, he ordered, "Eyes on me."

I opened my hooded gaze, trying to catch my bearings.

He took a long, hard look at me and spoke with conviction,

"I'm the man who claims your ass. The one who makes love to you. The man that you need. The one you want… but mostly…"

I'd be lying if I said I didn't feel the same when he swept the hair away from my eyes.

Until he professed, "I'm the man who thought he was falling in love with you, but that's not it at all."

My eyebrows pinched together.

"No, you see, I'm the man who's always been in love with you, Noelle."

And just like that…

My mind was thrown back to the last time I saw him.

CHAPTER 25

NOELLE: THEN

By the look on his face, whatever he was going to say to me would hurt.

"You're scaring me," I voiced, my tone feeling scared. "What's going on?"

We were sitting in my living room a few weeks after graduation.

"Are you okay?"

"I will be."

"What does that mean?"

"It means I'm finally doing it."

"Doing what?"

"Opening my own business."

I lit up, standing. "That's great! Your father agreed to—"

"I'm leaving town, Elle."

I jerked back. "What do you mean?"

He stood, pulling me into a tight hug as he held me so close to his chest that I could feel his rapidly beating heart hammering against mine.

"I want you to go with me."

"Go with you where?"

He looked deep into my eyes. "To start a new life."

The certainty in his tone broke my heart like he'd already made his decision.

I knew this wouldn't be easy, saying goodbye never was, but we'd make it through this.

We were best friends.

"Elle." He pressed his lips against mine, rubbing them back and forth along my soft mouth.

I thought I was going to die.

I felt like I was dying.

He repeated for what felt like the millionth time, "You know I can't stay here."

"Why not?"

"I need to do this for me."

I winced for a second before responding, "That's not fair."

"None of this is fair."

This wasn't supposed to be this hard. This was on constant repeat in my head for the past few weeks. He'd been different, and he wouldn't tell me why.

Now I knew…

He was planning on leaving and trying to figure out how to tell me.

Or worse, how do get me to leave with him, which he knew I wouldn't.

Why is he doing this to me?

Inhaling a quick breath, he lifted his hand to the side of my face like he was trying to memorize it. His green eyes locked with mine, and it was the first time I realized how white they'd get when he was upset.

"Don't cry, Elle."

It was only then I realized I was crying.

We were only eighteen years old and had our whole lives ahead of us.

He kissed my lips, desperately hanging on by a very thin thread. "Please, come with me."

I didn't know what to expect from this goodbye, but nothing could have prepared me for what happened next. It was by far the most devastating moment for me out of all this. I was being pulled in two different directions, and for the life of me, I stood there silently praying I was making the right one.

"What if I ask you not to go?"

His eyes widened, waiting for I don't know what.

For the first time, my heart wanted one thing, and my mind wanted the other.

I battled a war of what felt right but could also be wrong.

My mind spun on an endless loop of what was I doing…

He must have sensed my hesitation, and I laid my hand over his heart. "What if we started our lives now? Here? Together?"

"Noelle…"

Life was full of choices, and all it took was one decision to change the path of our lives.

"Who's my girl?" He kissed her again, harder that time. "You're my good girl. Come with me."

The truth was, I was ready to throw it all away…

For him.

The immediate relief I felt when he kissed me with such passion and devotion was like nothing I could begin to describe. It was as if my world was back in place, and everything was as it should be.

I lost myself in that kiss.

There.

With him.

In his arms.

With this body pressed against mine.

Our hearts against one another.

153

Nicholas's pride was his biggest strength and his greatest weakness. His determination would get him far, that much I was positive of. I knew he'd made all his dreams come true. It was how he was made. When he set his mind to something, there was no telling him no. He'd make it happen, no matter what or who tried to block him.

A huge part of me wanted to move with him, but I had my own dreams too. I wanted to accomplish so much; I just never imagined it would be without him.

Not in this town.

The one I loved so much.

The one I wanted a future in.

Raise a family in.

The one I finally had a life in.

For a few seconds, I sincerely thought that maybe I was getting through to him. That he was going to choose me in the end, us, and this would be the beginning of our fairy tale.

Until he expressed, "I'm sorry, I can't."

I lost.

Maybe in another life, we could have been together.

Maybe it just wasn't the right time for us.

Maybe we just weren't meant to be.

Maybe…

Maybe…

Maybe…

I repeated his same words, "I'm sorry, I can't." In reference to leaving with him.

"Why?" he instantly argued.

I could see his anger fueling.

"How can you ask me to leave? You know how much this place means to me. Your whole family is here. Why would you want to leave?"

"You know why."

"Ugh! You can't just ask me to leave with you and expect me to say yes. That's not fair."

Neither one of us said anything for I don't know how long. Both of us were lost in our own thoughts. The future played out in front of me, almost like a crystal ball.

I didn't like what I saw.

What I felt.

It was awful.

I didn't have my best friend.

"Please don't go," I begged, needing to get through to him.

"Please come with me," he pleaded, wanting to get through to me too.

Again, silence.

It was truly deafening and loud at the same time.

He kissed me.

Softly.

Affectionately.

It was a goodbye kiss.

The one you see in movies.

Read about in books.

I wanted to understand him, but I couldn't, and I hated him for that. The emotions were conflicting, each and everyone.

"Please don't do this…" I proceeded, my will to not leave with him dwindling.

I didn't think it was over.

Even after he left.

Even after I realized much later that this would be the last time we'd see each other for the next thirteen years, yet he still didn't say…

"I love you."

CHAPTER 26

NOELLE: NOW

"I should have said it then to you," he confessed like he knew exactly where my mind went.

He didn't hesitate to grip the back of my legs and carry me inside the gingerbread house.

Talk about full circle.

It had a heater, along with an obscene amount of food and blankets. He turned it into a cozy place for us to hang in. What a perfect way to spend Christmas Eve.

He set me down on the table he built for me with his own bare hands. Once I was sitting between his legs, he kissed me.

"I'm so sorry, Elle," he coaxed between kissing. "For hurting your perfect heart."

"I know."

And I did.

"I'm sorry too."

And I was.

"I wish we could go back and change things to not have to lose all that time."

"I wouldn't change anything."

"Really?"

He smiled against my mouth. "It led us to this place in time where I know without a shadow of a doubt that you're my person."

I smiled back onto his lips. "Like your soulmate?"

"Like my everything." He grabbed my face. "It's crazy because I knew in the back of my mind that it's always been you. I didn't even realize how much everyone else knew too until I arrived here. I never realized how much everyone could see it. My friend Dan, who has never seen us together, knew just by hearing me talk about you."

My eyes rimmed with tears.

"He told me to just give in to you, into us, and it's been the best decision I've ever made. You've made me realize just how much is missing in my life. My family. You. A puppy."

I giggled. "He is awfully cute."

"I realize now that this is not only where I need to be but also where I want to be."

"What are you saying?"

"I'm saying… I love you, I love you, I love you…"

My eyes widened as he leaned back, unbuckled his belt, unzipped his pants, and freed his cock. Grabbing my hips next, he lifted me and pulled down my overalls.

In one quick, sudden motion, my chest was pressed against the table, and he thrust deep inside me.

"Yes…"

I savored in the feel only he could give me. His hands made their way down to my ass, guiding my movements, finding a rhythm that drove me into a wild frenzy. I was overpowered by the feelings he stirred all around me, and I allowed the familiar ache to take over.

He placed my face between his hands and peered at me adoringly. "No more bullshit between us, Elle. You're mine."

I came, and he growled, "You're going to let me back in."

I panted, "You are in."

He didn't let up on his rough thrusts. "You're going to not only give me your heart, your soul, your friendship, and pussy, but you're also going to give me your ass... and you know what else?"

I nodded, finally giving him what we both wanted.

NICHOLAS

"The taste of you, the scent of you, the feel of you, nothing compares to you." My calloused hands roamed up her bare thighs, never taking my eyes off her beautiful face. "You're the best thing that's ever happened to me."

Her legs trembled.

Her body shook.

Her hips swayed without realizing she was doing so.

"You're my sweet, perfect Elle."

Our eyes connected.

What started off tender became urgent and demanding.

Branding her with my heated gaze.

Searing her.

Consuming her.

"No one has ever looked at me the way you do," she breathed out.

"No one has ever loved you the way I do." I locked eyes with her heated stare that mirrored mine, huskily groaning, "I can still taste your sweet little cunt in my mouth."

Roughly gripping her thighs, I thrust into her harder.

She gasped a heady breath, and I took my time, savoring the feel of her.

Inch by inch, making her pant beneath me as I descended toward my final destination, working her into a frenzy.

Kissing.

Licking.

Biting the side of her long, dainty neck.

Inhaling her addicting scent of arousal mixed with the sweet smell of her pussy. Finally, ending my tantalizing torture with a kiss on her mouth. I continued my assault on her G-spot, knowing precisely where she liked it.

So deep.

So hard.

So fucking good.

"Nicholas..." she purred out my name, fisting her hand in my hair, using the other to support her weight.

I glided my tongue in her hungry mouth.

Her eyes closed, and her head fell back against my shoulder, grinding her hips in a back-and-forth motion. Her cum dripped down my balls and legs.

"Oh God..."

"Oh, you like that, do you? Where, Elle? Right here?"

I witnessed her unraveling from the inside out, possessing every last fiber of her being. I wanted to see what I was eliciting through her stare, only fueling my desire to have her watch me make her come, and she moaned in response.

Shaking.

Coming.

Surrendering.

Her body shook so violently, like a volcano ready to erupt from the pressure, the pleasure.

Seconds later, she came hard, screaming out, "Nicholas!"

I let her ride out her orgasm, and then I came deep inside her. Through burning eyes, I took what I wanted before she could reply, desperately kissing her.

I confessed, "You're the first gift I ever wished for."

In which she confessed back, "I love you too."

CHAPTER 27

NICHOLAS

"Good morning, Elle," I groaned from behind her, wrapping my arms around her waist.

She was looking out the window at the snow falling on the ground.

"Merry Christmas," I stated, kissing her shoulder.

"Merry Christmas." She smiled. "If you're hungry, I can make you something to eat."

"Oh, I'm starving."

She tried turning around, but I caught her wrist.

"For you. I'm always starved for you."

Noelle Woods had always been my biggest weakness and my greatest strength.

So many what-ifs raced through my mind.

So many consequences and scenarios that could still happen.

So many choices that could be right or wrong.

Unable to help myself, I reached over and caressed the side of her face.

She leaned into my embrace like she had been waiting for me to do so.

Her eyes closed, melting into my touch.

"Don't you want to see what Santa brought you for Christmas?"

She chuckled. "Of course, but we're due at the bakery soon. We need to get started on the baking."

"Whatever you say, Miss Woods."

"Oh, I'm back to Miss Woods, is it?"

One thing I was sure of in this second was that her guard was coming down. She knew when I was with her, there was nowhere else I wanted to be.

"Nicholas..."

My heart sped up, hearing my name roll off her tongue.

The smell and feel of her were all around me, making me burn with desire to claim every last inch of her heart, body, and soul. I wanted to capture this moment and hold on to it for as long as I could.

I wanted to remember her just like this.

The only gift I wanted in my arms on Christmas morning.

For me.

Mine.

"Why aren't you in my bed? I don't like to wake up alone."

Her breathing hitched when my thumb pulled on her bottom lip. My hand suddenly moved to grip the back of her neck and bring her toward me.

"You make me laugh, smile, and feel like a kid again," I declared. "You make me want to be a better man. Do you have any idea how much you affect me? From your eyes, to your ridiculous fucking giggle, to the way you calm me. The way you see me, the way you've always seen me. You fill this void, a hole in my heart that I felt growing up until I met you in the library one random afternoon. No one has ever been able to come close to how I feel when you're in my arms." I paused to let my words sink in. "For years, I tried to break that hold you've always had over me, but I couldn't. And the truth is, Elle, I didn't want to let it go. I didn't want to let you go. Because at the end of the day, I learned what it felt like to be your best friend, and I wouldn't change that for anything."

Her lips parted to say something. "Do you want your gift?"

"How about we gift each other later and get started on eating your cookies?"

She threw her head back, laughing. Before she could leave to get dressed, I kissed her.

I devoured her, beckoning her to do the same, her lips to open for me. She released a soft moan as my tongue slid into her mouth. I'd always been a man of few words. To me, actions always spoke much louder and clearer than any sentence ever could. Yet there I was, laying it all out for her.

Word by word.

Sentence by sentence.

Making my thoughts and emotions known.

Slowly easing back, I added, "Go get dressed. Wear something festive for me." I pecked her mouth one last time before releasing her.

She smiled and ran into the bathroom.

An hour later, she was dressed in a reindeer getup with knee-high boots and thigh-high stockings. I resisted the urge to bend her over the table again and remind her who drives her sleigh, but she insisted we needed to get going to get done in time for the town to make their way through.

Several hours later, we just finished cooking another batch of chocolate chips when I asked, "What was your major in college?"

"A double bachelor in business and finances with a minor in accounting."

"Wow. Two bachelor's degrees. That must have been a lot of studying." I nodded, licking the batter off her face.

Did I forget to mention that the second we started baking, she came out wearing nothing but a Grinch apron with stockings and boots. We spent the first hour of the morning making a mess with cake and batter mix in places where it probably shouldn't go.

"I had to prove to your grandfather that I could handle this place."

"When did you decide to go to work for him?"

"Pretty early on. Part of me always wanted to take it over."

"What happened after college?"

"I worked my life away until you came back in it."

I smiled, winking at her. "Ditto."

"So no women in your life?"

"They were meaningless."

"I'm sure they didn't think that."

"They knew what they were getting themselves into. I never lied about any expectations when it came to them."

She smiled. "You always know the right things to say."

"It's called honesty."

"Okay, Mr. Honesty, how many kids do you want?"

I jerked back, surprised by her question.

"I mean, we never talked about those kinds of things, so now I'm curious."

I responded, "Three."

"Three?" Her eyes widened.

"How many do you want?"

She ignored my question.

"Do you want a boy or a girl?"

"I'd like a baby girl who looks exactly like you."

She blushed.

"I keep finding myself envisioning a life with you."

"What kind of life?"

She looked down at her stomach.

"You'd be an amazing mother."

"I'm not so sure about that. I don't think I'm very maternal."

"You're the most loving person I know." I wrapped my arms around her waist from behind her to help her with the cookie dough in front of her.

"This is very Patrick Swayzee of you in Ghost except here comes Santa Claus wasn't playing in the background."

We'd been listening to Christmas music, and I'd never be able to hear Rudolph the red nose reindeer without envisioning Noelle on her knees in front of me, wearing her reindeer getup.

"This is where I belong."

CHAPTER 28

NICHOLAS

"I can't believe you're making me do this..." I complained, looking in the mirror.

"Oh, come on... you look so cute, though."

There I was, wearing The Grinch costume.

"Now, if you can stand at the door and hand out cookies, please and thank you."

"Oh, how lucky."

She giggled, running away before I could catch her.

For the next several hours, I played the role of The Grinch until I couldn't take it anymore and had to take the damn thing off. Thankfully, I was about to get Noelle on the skating rink before it opened. I may or may not have ordered the staff to leave us alone so that I could fuck her in the rink.

A fantasy I didn't know I had until I saw her on skates in her Rudolph outfit. She was the cutest reindeer I'd ever seen. I told her to run and chased her around the rink wearing The Grinch costume before I proceeded to get on my knees and show her a very merry Christmas.

She loved every second of it.

By the time we got back to the bakery, the town was packed, and I made my way through the crowd, looking for my family. I knew they'd be around. They usually like to stay close to the bakery. The Saint Clair's had one hell of a sweet tooth.

"Holly!" I called out, finding them where I thought.

"Nicholas!" She hugged me.

We spent the next hour just hanging out, shooting the shit about nothing in particular until I pulled my brother aside for a minute.

"What's up?" he questioned.

"I have a Christmas gift for you."

His eyebrows pinched together. "We're exchanging presents?"

"You knew better than that, Felix. Christmas is all about giving, not receiving."

"Look whose heart grew three sizes."

"Shut up and just open it," I chuckled, handing him a box.

"You brought me a shirt?"

"You're worse than Noelle. Just open the damn thing and find out."

He did as he was told, coming face-to-face with what I had in store for him.

"You're joking?" he asked with a stunned expression I'd never seen on his face.

"Not at all. Merry Christmas, Felix."

With wide eyes, he asked, "Does Dad know?"

"Yeah." I nodded. "I told him about it this morning."

"And he's okay with it?"

"Why wouldn't he be okay with it? His two sons running Mistletoe Town."

"You're being serious?"

"Yes," I reassured. "I don't have the time or the desire to run the town, especially when I'm relocating my business here. I still have projects to finish up, but I'll start the process. I want to stay behind the scenes. I can attend the meetings and the events, but I do not need the day-to-day; that's where you come in."

Still with wide eyes, he added, "I can't believe this."

"Well, believe it." I extended out my hand to shake his. "We're now partners."

He took one look at my gesture and grabbed my hand instead, pulling me into a tight hug.

I repeated, smiling. "Merry Christmas, Felix."

"Merry Christmas, Nicholas."

"Now, this is the sight I want to see," our father exclaimed, walking up behind us.

He wrapped his arms around us.

It was a good feeling, and the truth was...

My heart did grow three sizes, and this was a story about a man who found joy in giving to others, especially when they deserved it. My brother knew the town like the back of his hand, so it was logical to bring him on. He worked his ass off for our grandfather.

This town did bring out the best in me once I stopped fighting it. I don't know if it was Christmas or just plain old age, but I found the magic that lay within.

With the shove from my grandfather, I got everything I ever wanted.

My dad shook my hand before doing the same as Felix and pulled me into another tight hug.

"I love you, son."

"I love you too, Dad."

I did the only thing left for me to do. I drove Noelle up to the woods where we'd see all the Christmas lights in town.

As soon as we got up there, she beamed. "I love it here."

"Me too."

"Now I can have my way with you."

I grinned, loving the way her eyes lit up from my simple response. I shook off the sentiment, grabbing her hand again.

"You see, Miss Woods. I discovered the love of a woman and its power over me."

I backed her up into the tree, pressing her up against it with my right arm locking her in place by the side of her face. It was then she noticed we were under a mistletoe.

"You had the love of a girl back then, too," she recapped, kissing down the side of my neck.

"I have your gifts for you."

She peered up at my eyes through her long lashes.

"As in more than one?"

"Open it and find out."

I handed her an envelope first. "What is this?"

"I'm just doing my job." I grinned.

Once she saw the document in her hand, she sucked in air, startled by what she was seeing.

"Just call me Santa Claus."

"Oh my God! You gave me the bakery?"

I kissed her. "Now you own a piece of the town you love so much."

"I can't believe this…"

"You deserve it."

I continued my gentle torture for a few more seconds until I handed her the next present.

"Nicholas, how are you going to top this?"

"Let's find out." I grinned again.

When she pulled out a diamond, her mouth dropped open.

In one swift motion, I dropped to my knees and professed, "I love you. I want to spend the rest of my life with you. Will you do me the honor of marrying me?"

She tackled me into the snow. "Of course!"

Our gazes stayed connected, her eyes showing me everything I wanted to hear.

Even after all these years, they still spoke volumes.

I pulled her closer to me by the nook of her neck, and she bit her bottom lip, enticing me.

"I love you," she whispered against my lips. "I love you so much. I love that you asked me here and under a mistletoe. It's perfect. You're perfect."

I grabbed the ring, sliding it down her finger. "I'm never losing you again."

"Wow! This is stunning."

"Only the best for my girl."

We stayed there on the hill until well after midnight enjoying this moment.

It was truly a merry Christmas to all and to all a good night.

CHAPTER 29

NICHOLAS

The following morning, I woke her up with my face between her legs. I aimed my fingers right against her G-spot once she was wet enough.

"Ahhhh…" she moaned out loud.

Her breathing elevated, showing me that I was getting to her. I slid my middle finger out from her hot cunt, loving the feel of her slickness against my callused fingers.

"That's how wet I make you," I growled.

I pushed my middle and ring fingers back into her pussy. Her body angled perfectly beneath mine. She melted against me, taking everything I was giving her and wanting more.

Wanting everything.

"Do you want me to make love to you?" I said between kisses. "Do you want me to make you come?" I urged, pushing my fingers deeper into her sweet spot.

She panted, "Right there."

"Where?" I cocked my head to the side, still not moving our lips apart. "Here?"

"Yes…"

"Tell me."

"I love you…"

Her juices slid down the palm of my hand. She was so close to coming apart.

She shuddered, her body quivering.

"One," I pointed out.

Not allowing her to recover, I took her clit into my mouth. Her body started to convulse all around my face. The hood of her clit pulled back, exposing her fucking bright red nub. All I had to do was take it into my mouth and suck.

Hard.

She was so fucking wet, I bathed in her salty, musky sweetness. Rubbing my face all over her pussy, I drenched my lips and my beard. I lapped at her, never taking my persistent tongue away from her clit, making her squirm to no avail.

Her juices dripped down my face, to my throat, and onto my chest, soaking my chest.

I loved hearing her moan.

Pant.

Her breath raced.

I loved the way she struggled to catch her bearings as my tongue danced from her clit to her opening and back to her clit again.

She literally fucked my face.

Coming over and over again.

"Two, three, and four," I teased the number of times I made her come on my tongue.

Sliding down the length of my body, she got down on her knees in front of me, pulling out my hard cock from my gym shorts. She licked off the pre-cum, then sucked the head into her mouth, taking me in inch by inch.

With her body beneath mine and my dick hovering above her mouth, I thrust in and out of her swollen lips from last night.

Her pouty mouth took my dick as I shoved it to the back of her throat, making her gag, spit falling down the sides of her face.

"Fuck... I need to be inside you."

Her eyes watered with tears, but she didn't let up. I enjoyed the feel of her lips wrapped around my cock and her taking every last inch I had to give. Removing my cock from her mouth with a pop, she aggressively sucked in the air that my dick denied her.

I didn't falter.

Grabbing her underneath the arms, I carried her up the length of my body. Then I slammed her down onto my cock in one swift, sudden movement.

"I want to fuck my fiancée, soon-to-be wife."

I took it easy on her at first, letting her get used to my size, knowing she was sore. Her mouth parted, and her soft, wet tongue peeked out. She bit her bottom lip while trying to keep her eyes open.

I took in her soft glow.

Her rosy cheeks.

The subtle sweat pooling at her temples.

I watched the way her tits bounced.

The way her back would curve.

How she arched just slightly at the last second of feeling my balls swaying against her ass cheeks.

I lay down on the bed with her now on top of me. She rode my dick slow and steady, and I let her feel like she was in control.

I smacked her ass hard, and her eyes widened in surprise and delight while I gripped onto her ass cheeks, making her ride me harder and faster.

Noelle loved to be manhandled and feel owned, and I gladly gave it to her. I clutched the back of her neck and brought her to me. She leaned forward, and I could feel her G-spot on the tip of my cock, causing me to groan in satisfaction.

Watching her ride my dick should be a sport in itself. My favorite show.

Mine.

She helplessly, breathlessly repeated, "Yes... yes... yes..."

A growl surfaced loud from deep within my chest. She was so tight it made my balls ache. Manipulating her clit with my fingers, her legs started to tremble, caging my body in. I thrust in and out of her, never letting up on fucking her. Grabbing onto her breasts, I roughly caressed her hard nipples.

The firmness of my grasp was evident from her bright red skin. I smacked it a few times, knowing it would leave a mark. I growled and held her down, moving her up and down on my cock until she begged me to stop.

Her pussy pulsated and clamped onto my cock, pushing me out of her wet, warm heat.

The way she would squirm.

The way she would hold her breath right before falling over the brink of ecstasy. Taking every last bit of pleasure she could.

"Nicholas Yes... yes..."

Coming with everything she had.

The way she took her pleasure with everything I made her feel.

My balls throbbed with the need to come from watching her climax.

"I love you," I groaned out, emptying my balls deep into her pussy.

She kissed all over my face, and we spent most of the morning in bed.

"What happens now?" she asked, looking up at me as she lay on my chest with Max on the other side of me.

"As half the owner of Mistletoe Town—"

"Wait?" She sat up. "Half?"

I smiled. "My brother and I now own it."

By the expression on her face, she was pleased with my answer. "That was very nice of you."

I shrugged. "It's a win-win."

"You didn't have to do that."

"I know, but I wanted to. The next step is to relocate my business here."

"I love that idea. I can bake you cookies, and you can come eat them on your lunch break." I kissed her.

"I'd love that. You know this is all because of you, right? You're the magic of Christmas."

"No, Nicholas. You have it all wrong." She moved to sit on my lap. "You're the magic. You've always been the magic."

"How do you figure?"

"Look how happy you've made everyone."

She had a point.

"I was just doing my part."

"Like Santa…" she teased.

"I've checked twice now. You're definitely on the naughty list."

"Well, my Grinch kind of lives there."

"What time does your dad land tomorrow?"

"Noon. He's bringing his girlfriend."

They decided to spend the holidays on an island.

"Does my dad know?"

"Of course."

"When did you ask his permission?"

"When I was delivering everyone's gifts," I laughed, holding my whole life in my arms.

For the first time in my life, I felt the true meaning of Christmas and what it felt like to be loved. I guess you could say I came around.

However, nobody needed to know that.

Because at the end of the day…

I did inherit this holiday.

EPILOGUE: TWO MONTHS LATER

NOELLE

In the blink of an eye, my life turned into everything I ever wanted.

"Oh shit…" I expressed, looking at the bright pink positive stick in my hand. "Oh God… Nicholas," I shouted.

It didn't take long for him to walk into the bathroom with what looked like a letter in his hand. His awestruck eyes went from the letter to the pregnancy test in my hand.

"Oh, wow…" He smiled wide. "A puppy and a baby… those are quite the gifts."

"Yeah…" That was all I could muster.

I mean, I was happy.

Stunned but happy.

"Why are you looking at me like that?" I asked with caution.

It was only then that he handed me the letter.

There in front of my eyes was the reason he was acting so funny and nonchalant about me being pregnant.

I couldn't believe it.

I wasn't the magic.

Neither was Nicholas.

Nor Max.

Or the baby.

Nope.

It was the person I least expected but couldn't have been more grateful to.

NICHOLAS

My fucking grandfather…

He was either a wizard or a psychic or shit at this point, maybe he was the one pulling the strings. That was the only explanation to the letter in my hands that Alfred just delivered to me that read…

> *I'M ALWAYS RIGHT.*
>
> *YOU'RE WELCOME FOR THE TOWN, THE WIFE, AND THE BABY…*
>
> *YOU CAN THANK ME LATER.*
>
> *P.S. I WAS GOING TO LEAVE MISTLETOE TOWN TO YOU AND YOUR BROTHER, BUT I FIGURED IT'D BE BEST IF YOU DID THAT INSTEAD.*
>
> *LIKE I SAID, I'M ALWAYS RIGHT.*

And that indeed…

He was.

The end…

COMING SOON

To find out what's next from Monica, please visit her website at authormrobinson.com

ALSO BY M. ROBINSON

THE BILLION-AIRE MEN

Bossy Billionaire

Vicious Tycoon

Filthy Mogul

BECKHAM DYNASTY

Tempting Enemy

Perfect Enemy

Sinful Enemy

SECOND CHANCE SERIES

Second Chance Contract

Second Chance Vow

Second Chance Scandal

Second Chance Love

Second Chance Rival

Second Chance Mine

ANGSTY ROM-COM

The Kiss

The Fling

MAFIA/ORGANIZED CRIME ROMANCE

El Diablo

El Santo

El Pecador

Sinful Arrangement

Mafia Casanova: Co-written with Rachel Van Dyken

Falling for the Villain: Co-written with Rachel Van Dyken

SMALL TOWN ROMANCE

Complicate Me

Forbid Me

Undo Me

Crave Me

She Was Mine First

SINGLE DAD / NANNY ROMANCE

Choosing Us

Choosing You

ENEMIES TO LOVERS ROMANCE

Hated You Then

Love You Now

MC ROMANCE

Road to Nowhere

Ends Here

MMA FIGHTER ROMANCE

Lost Boy

ROCK STAR ROMANCE

From the First Verse

'Til the Last Lyric

BUNDLES

ABOUT THE AUTHOR

M. Robinson is the Wall Street Journal and USA Today Bestselling author of more than thirty novels in Contemporary Romance and Romantic Suspense. Crowned the "Queen of Angst" by her loyal readers, you'll feel the cut of her pen slicing through your heart as your soul bleeds upon the words of her stories with each turn of the page.

Most notably known for the Good Ol' Boys, M's newest venture has graced her with the #1 Bestseller on Apple Books with Second Chance Contract. The Second Chance Men are powerful, intelligent and will sweep you off your feet and leave you weak in the knees–every woman's wildest dreams.

M. lives the boat life along the Gulf Coast of Florida with her two puppies and real life book boyfriend, the inspiration for all her filthy talking alphas, Bossman.

When she isn't in the cave writing her next epic love story, you can usually spot her mad-dashing through Target or in the drive-thru of Starbucks, refueling. Yes, she's a self-proclaimed shopaholic, but only if she's spending Bossman's money.

You can follow M, Ted, Marley, and Bossman on Facebook, Instagram, and her absolute favorite social platform-TikTok.

Printed in Great Britain
by Amazon